WORLD WAR II

The First Bloody Battles

 **Marshall Cavendish**
Benchmark
New York

D1442674

Library of Congress Cataloging-in-Publication Data

The first bloody battles.
    p. cm. -- (World War II)
  Includes bibliographical references and index.
  Summary: "Covers the outbreak of World War II from 1939 to 1941 including Germany's blitzkrieg tactics, the bombing raids on London, the North African campaign, the Battle of the Atlantic, and the attack on Pearl Harbor"--Provided by publisher.
  ISBN 978-0-7614-4946-1
  1. World War, 1939-1945--Campaigns--Juvenile literature.

  D743.7.F57 2011
  940.54'2--dc22
                              2010008623

Senior Editor: Deborah Grahame-Smith
Publisher: Michelle Bisson
Art Director: Anahid Hamparian
Series Designer: Bill Smith Group

PICTURE CREDITS
Associated Press: 4, 10, 17, 20, 42, 52, 87, 90, 101
Library of Congress: 24 (National Photo Company Collection), 29 (U.S. Army Signal Corps), 79 (Official U.S. Navy photo from OWI), 95 (U.S. Army Air Forced, from Royal Air Force, Washington, D.C.), 96 (Office of War Information Photograph Collection), 109 (Harris & Ewing), 116 (Alfred T. Palmer), 122 (U.S. Navy, Office of Public Relations)
United States Coast Guard: 89 (Jack January)
National Archives and Records: 114
Robert Hunt Library: Cover, 32, 48, 60, 74
Shutterstock: 8 (Torsten Lorenz), 25 (Torsten Lorenz), 37 (Engin Hakki Bilgin), 38 (Wolfgang Amri), 44 (Sergey Kamshylin), 86 (markrhiggins),

Additional imagery provided by U.S. Army, Joseph Gary Sheahan, 1944, Dreamstime.com, Shutterstock.com.

Printed in Malaysia (T)
135642

Contents

▶ A German unit that fought in Poland joins a victory parade on October 5, 1939.

1

Germany's Blitzkrieg Victories, 1939 to 1940

KEY PEOPLE	KEY PLACES	
Charles de Gaulle	Ardennes, France	Paris, France
Erwin Rommel	Dunkirk, France	Vichy, France
Gerd von Rundstedt	Maginot Line, France	Warsaw, Poland

Between September 1939 and June 1940, Germany invaded country after country in Europe. These attacks used tactics known as *Blitzkrieg* (lightning war). They made use of fast-moving tanks supported by bombers. In this way, German forces defeated their enemies in weeks.

Poland was Hitler's first target. By signing a nonaggression pact with the Soviet Union, Hitler ensured that the Soviets would not help Poland. But Britain and France had promised to fight to defend Poland. Hitler was gambling that Poland would fall quickly. In this, Hitler was proved correct. By mid-September 1939, Poland had been mostly overrun by the German army. France was still mobilizing its forces and could not intervene.

The Conquest of Poland

On August 31, 1939, Germans faked an attack on a German radio station on the Polish border. Instead of Polish troops, the attackers were German inmates from concentration camps in disguise. But this incident was the excuse for the German invasion of Poland.

The German invasion, code-named *Fall Weiss* or Case White, began on September 1, 1939. The initial attack was made by fifty-five divisions of German troops. These forces were arranged into two large formations called Army Group North and Army Group South. Striking from different directions, they were to meet in the area of the Polish capital, Warsaw. Then, they would encircle most of the Polish armies on the western border.

Opposing the Germans were thirty Polish divisions—not all fully ready on September 1. These forces were spread along Poland's western and northern borders between Germany and East Prussia. Their goal was to protect Poland's important industrial centers. By spreading their troops out along a front of more than 1,250 miles (2,012 km), the Poles unwittingly gave the Germans a key advantage.

This map shows the German invasion of Poland in September 1939. German attacks can be seen in orange; Russian movements are shown in blue.

The Polish troops, without tanks and mechanized transport, could not move quickly to counterattack. Unlike the Germans, the Poles relied on horse-mounted cavalry. Horses were no match against modern military equipment. The Germans quickly punched through the Polish lines.

In addition, the Polish air force lacked the modern aircraft, facilities, and fuel to seriously oppose the *Luftwaffe* or German air force. The Germans sent more than 1,000 bombers and large numbers of fighters. These aircraft first destroyed the Polish air force. Then they supported the ground attack by bombing communication centers, pockets of resistance, and troops. One type of dive bomber, the Ju 87 Stuka, proved especially effective.

Although the Poles fought back with great courage, they were quickly outmaneuvered. The Germans broke through the Polish lines on the border and within days were close to Warsaw. They finished encircling the Polish forces by mid-September. The trapped forces fought hard, but after a week some 170,000 men surrendered. As the Polish struggled to regroup their remaining troops, the Germans continued to push eastward.

The trapped forces fought hard, but after a week some 170,000 men surrendered.

Then, on September 17, as Stalin and Hitler had agreed earlier, the Soviet Union sent its army into Poland. In a few days, Red Army troops linked up with German forces. Polish leaders fled to Romania on September 18. In 1940 they established a government-in-exile in Britain.

Poland ceased to exist as an independent country. Under the terms of the German-Soviet Delimitation Pact, Poland was split between Germany and the Soviet Union. The countries Estonia, Latvia, and Lithuania came under Soviet control, and parts of Warsaw and Lublin went to Germany.

Fighting continued until October 2. By that time Hitler's forces had captured 690,000 Poles with the loss of 10,500 men killed and 30,000 wounded. The Red Army took 217,000 prisoners. Around 66,000 Poles were killed.

About 100,000 Polish troops escaped to Romania. Many of these men made their way to Britain. These troops formed the core of the Polish army in exile. Much later, they would return to the continent of Europe and make their presence felt.

BLITZKRIEG

Blitzkrieg (literally translated as "lightning war") was a new form of warfare. It relied on powerful attacks by tanks, cooperating closely with aircraft. Germany's Blitzkrieg offensives proved highly successful in 1939 and 1940.

This form of highly mobile warfare evolved as a reaction to the war on the western front in World War I. The fighting in that war was characterized by little movement. Troops fought from trenches, but their losses were high.

However, in spring 1918, specialist German storm trooper units broke the deadlock. They attacked suddenly, after artillery attacks that were short but heavy. The troops struck at weak points in the British and French trenches. These German attackers went around the strongest pockets of resistance and penetrated deep behind the front lines. This tactic caused massive confusion and disorder to the defenders. But the strategy was not enough to save Germany from defeat. Several reasons contributed to the failure, but two were important for the future development of Blitzkrieg. The artillery was not able to keep up with the fast-moving troops, and the foot soldiers eventually became physically exhausted.

World War I also saw new types of weapons, including tanks. Tanks combined engines, armor, and heavy guns. These would let the artillery support move rapidly, keeping up with the leading edge of the attack. Meanwhile, ground-attack aircraft could also bomb and shoot at targets on the battlefield, clearing the way for the tanks and infantry. A final technology, radio, let the three elements of attack—tanks, aircraft, and infantry—coordinate. Together and react quickly to any new threat.

Between the wars, the theory of Blitzkrieg was developed. Officers from several countries wrote books discussing the concept. But German officers embraced Blitzkrieg and developed tanks and aircraft especially for this style of fighting.

Blitzkrieg worked well against Poland and France in 1939 and 1940. But the tactic had its weaknesses. Both invasions were short campaigns against unprepared enemies. Even so, the German armored formations were pushed to their limits. Mechanical failures were common, and supplies were running short by the time the campaigns ended. Then, against the Soviet Union, quick victory proved impossible. The vast distances of the Soviet Union highlighted the problem of supply.

As the war went on, Germany's enemies, in part due to greater industrial output, gradually kept the Luftwaffe from holding control of the air. At the same time, the Allies gradually learned to fight in the same style as the Germans. They developed effective tank divisions and antitank weapons. They were able to halt German attacks and counterattack quickly.

France and Britain had tried to help Poland when Germany first attacked. Both countries declared war on Germany on September 3. In an effort to help the Poles, France launched a small attack on the German border. The French attack was halfhearted and made little progress. On September 13, the French accepted that Poland's defeat was inevitable and halted their attack. The fighting had not caused any significant inconvenience to the Germans in the west.

The Phony War

For seven months after the defeat of Poland, there was little military activity along Germany's western front. A U. S. senator nicknamed this period as the Phony War. The Germans called it the *Sitzkrieg* (sitting war). In France, the war became known as the *Drole de Guerre* (funny war).

In September 1939, the British Expeditionary Force (BEF) arrived in France. This was a force of 160,000 troops and 24,000 vehicles. They moved in to northeastern France and joined the French army in the front line. At the end of September, the British and French troops outnumbered the German troops who opposed them by two to one. There was the brief chance for an Allied offensive. But the French claimed they were not yet ready for an attack. Soon after the defeat of Poland, most of the German army moved to the western front with one hundred divisions and more men arriving each day. The Allies soon lost their chance.

On October 9, 1939 Hitler ordered plans for an invasion of France. Meanwhile, the Allied commanders struggled to define their strategy. Neither Belgium nor the Netherlands would allow British or French troops on their soil. They feared this would provoke a German invasion. The British and French, therefore, decided to do nothing until a German invasion of the Low Countries (Belgium, the Netherlands, and Luxembourg) had taken place. Then they would move into Belgium and hold positions along the Dyle River. This maneuver would take eight days to complete. Thus, from the beginning the British and French allowed the Germans to choose the time and place when the fighting would begin. The Phony War ended in the spring of 1940 when other events in northern Europe began.

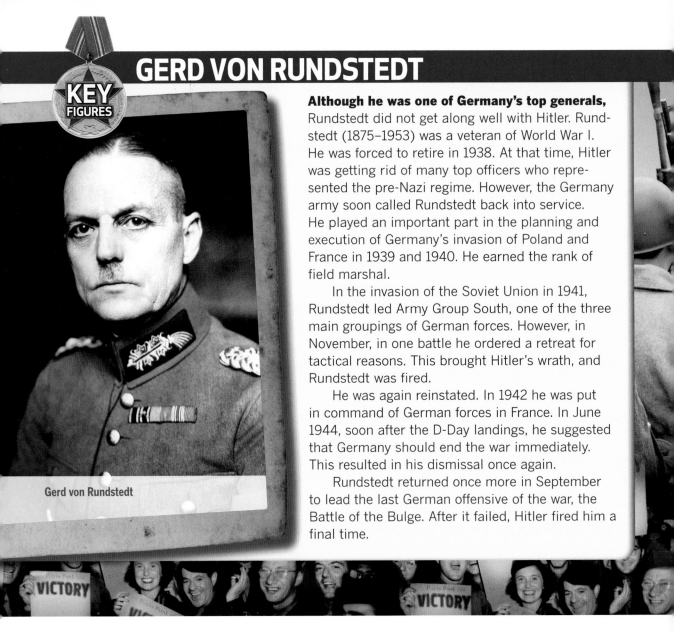

GERD VON RUNDSTEDT

Although he was one of Germany's top generals, Rundstedt did not get along well with Hitler. Rundstedt (1875–1953) was a veteran of World War I. He was forced to retire in 1938. At that time, Hitler was getting rid of many top officers who represented the pre-Nazi regime. However, the Germany army soon called Rundstedt back into service. He played an important part in the planning and execution of Germany's invasion of Poland and France in 1939 and 1940. He earned the rank of field marshal.

In the invasion of the Soviet Union in 1941, Rundstedt led Army Group South, one of the three main groupings of German forces. However, in November, in one battle he ordered a retreat for tactical reasons. This brought Hitler's wrath, and Rundstedt was fired.

He was again reinstated. In 1942 he was put in command of German forces in France. In June 1944, soon after the D-Day landings, he suggested that Germany should end the war immediately. This resulted in his dismissal once again.

Rundstedt returned once more in September to lead the last German offensive of the war, the Battle of the Bulge. After it failed, Hitler fired him a final time.

Gerd von Rundstedt

Denmark and Norway Overrun

Iron is a vital material for any country in wartime. Germany received about sixty-six percent of its iron ore from Sweden through Norwegian ports. Norway and Sweden were neutral countries. In spring 1940, the Allied leaders decided to cut off the flow of iron. The British naval forces rescued a group of Allied sailors being held prisoner on a German supply ship in the waters of Norway. Norway complained, but the British argued that the German supply ship had been in the same waters. Then, The British began to lay mines in Norwegian waters. Hitler decided to invade Denmark and Norway. The operation began on April 9. Denmark, which had few military resources, was overrun in a day.

The fighting in Norway took longer. The Germans sent a powerful army group, including paratroopers, supported by the Luftwaffe and Germany's entire navy. Troops landed at several Norwegian ports. British warships

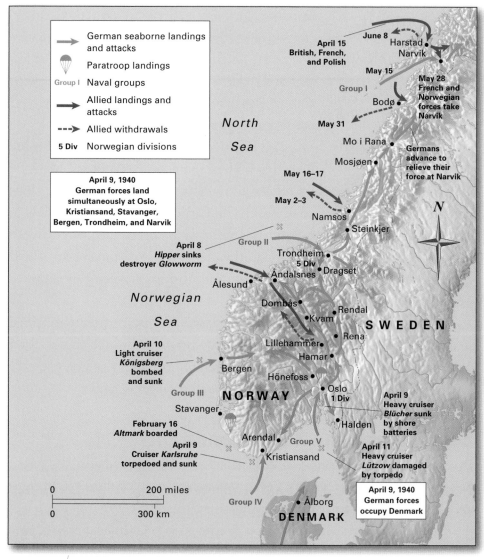

The German invasion of Denmark and Norway in April and May, 1940. Despite heavy losses at sea, German forces eventually took control of both countries.

inflicted heavy losses on the Germany navy, but the invasion continued. British and French attempted to land troops in central Norway to hold back the Germans. But these attempts were futile, and the Allied forces had to evacuate by mid-June. By that time, the Germans had invaded France, and Norway was almost forgotten.

The British and French forces totaled more than two million men and 3,600 tanks. Many of these tanks were superior to those of the Germans. However, the Allies split their tanks up into small groups and spread them across the whole front.

By early May, Germany was ready to invade France. Some 2.5 million troops were organized in three army groups along the border stretching from tne North Sea to Switzerland. The Germans concentrated their tank forces in a narrow section of the Belgian border. King Leopold III commanded 600,000 undertrained troops. Along with 400,000 Dutch army troops, the army also lacked modern equipment.

The British and French forces totaled more than two million men and 3,600 tanks. Many of these tanks were superior to those of the Germans. However, the Allies split their tanks up into small groups and spread them across the whole front. The French had 1,400 fighter aircraft and the British 290, but many of these were inferior to those of the Luftwaffe. The cornerstone of the Allied defense was the Maginot Line, a string of fortifications along the Franco-German border.

The German invasion of France was based on a powerful attack in the center. This armor-led attack would push westward through the wooded Ardennes in southern Belgium and Luxembourg. Many senior generals felt the plan was too risky, but Hitler ordered it put into action.

Belgium and the Netherlands Fall

On May 10, 1940, the attack began. German aircraft attacked airfields across Belgium and the Netherlands. Paratroopers landed to capture key bridges and airfields. German panzers and infantry charged across the border in the Netherlands and Belgium. In a daring move, German paratroopers captured the Belgian border fortress of Eben Emael, which guarded crossing points on the Albert Canal. This was a key defensive position. Its loss forced the Belgian army to fall back to the Dyle Line, the defensive position along the Dyle River. The plan had been for the BEF and French troops to advance and link up with the Belgian troops there. But as they advanced, Allied troops found the roads crowded with refugees trying to get away from the invaders.

On May 14, the Netherlands surrendered after the Luftwaffe destroyed much of Rotterdam's business district. The Dutch royal family escaped to Britain. Allied defenses forward of the Dyle Line collapsed. By May 15 the Belgians, British, and French were able to stop the Germans along the banks of the Dyle. But more German forces were joining in the fight.

> *On May 14, the Netherlands surrendered after the Luftwaffe destroyed much of Rotterdam's business district.*

Eban Emael

The Belgians considered their fortress of Eban Emael invincible. It was a complex of concrete and steel gun emplacements linked by underground tunnels. Yet it fell in just a few hours on May 10, 1940. Germany's generals needed to capture the position in order to cross the Albert Canal, Belgium's main line of defense.

Speed was essential, so a conventional attack was rejected. Instead, a small force of paratroopers landed directly on the fortress by glider. Eighty paratroopers carried special explosive charges that could pierce the steel armor of the gun positions. The paratroopers rapidly disabled many of the fort's guns. The Belgian defenders were paralyzed. Instead of counterattacking, they remained underground.

The German paratroopers held the position until the next day, when they were relieved by German troops who had crossed the Albert Canal. The loss of Eban Emael and the canal shattered the Belgians' main plan of defense.

The Invasion of France

The swift German drive through Belgium and the Netherlands had drawn the BEF and a large French force into southern Belgium. It was at this point that the main German push began. The main attack was spearheaded by Germany's best panzer divisions with their five armored and three motorized divisions. They moved quickly through the heavily wooded Ardennes region, where there were very few defenders. They emerged in a gap between French emplacements on the Maginot Line and the Allied forces in southern Belgium. The German tanks met poorly trained troops that were attempting to hold the line at the Meuse River.

This main attack was spearheaded by Germany's best panzer divisions with their five armored and three motorized divisions.

Aided by powerful air attacks, the armored spearhead crossed the Meuse River. They broke through the surprised French defenses. By May 15 the German armor had opened a 50-mile (80-km) gap in the front. The Germans then turned to the north with their 2,200 tanks and armored vehicles. Their aim was to drive to the English Channel at Abbeville. By doing so, they would cut off the Allied troops holding the Dyle Line to the north.

The Allied response to this threat was two attempts to punch through the developing German corridor to the Channel. But these attacks proved to be too little, too late. The French Brigadier General Charles de Gaulle led his 4th Armored Division against the southern flank of the German advance. After three attacks under heavy air attack from the Germans, de Gaulle had to break off. Against the northern flank of the German

Against the northern flank of the German advance, the British also launched a ferocious armored counterattack.

advance, the British also launched a ferocious armored counterattack. This too was eventually defeated by General Erwin Rommel's 7th Panzer Division. On the same day, May 21, German tanks reached the coast. Now the Belgian army, the BEF, and a large French army were cut off from the rest of the French forces to the south. Meanwhile, those forces were trying to create a new defensive line along the Somme and Aisne rivers.

Evacuation at Dunkirk

The British Expeditionary Force was surrounded. They held an ever-shrinking defensive position. Since the BEF was, in effect, the entire British army, its loss would leave Britain defenseless. Therefore, on May 24, the British commander ordered the BEF to withdraw to the French port of Dunkirk. From there they would evacuate back to Britain.

On the same day, Hitler ordered his armored forces on the Channel coast to halt, just as they were about to take Dunkirk. Hitler's decision gave the British a much greater chance to escape. A huge collection of naval and civilian ships and boats sailed from Dover, England. The evacuation was code-named Dynamo. It began on May 26.

In Dunkirk and on nearby beaches, troops waited for ships to rescue them. They were constantly bombed and shot at by German aircraft. Allied troops fought to hold back German forces attempting to break through to the beaches. In the days between May 26 and June 4, an amazing 338,226 troops were rescued and brought to England. Most were British, but 113,000 were Belgian and French troops. Many Allied ships were sunk during the evacuation. Also, the British had left most of their heavy equipment behind.

The Fall of France

After Dunkirk, the Germans pushed for the total defeat of France. General Maxime Weygand, the new French commander, tried to organize a defense of Paris and the Maginot Line. But his troops were badly outnumbered and short of equipment. Most of all, their morale were badly shaken by the strength of the German attacks that seemed unstoppable.

The Luftwaffe had total air superiority. German planes could range far and wide, hitting troops and convoys on the roads. The planes also fired on columns of refugeees along the road.

Weygand ordered a defense of the Somme and Aisne rivers. He stressed that it was important "to stand fast on the Somme–Aisne Line and fight to the last there." The defenders fought hard. But the Germans were able to advance, breaking through and carving up the French positions. The Luftwaffe had total air superiority. German planes could range far and wide, hitting troops and convoys on the roads. The planes also fired on columns of refugeees along the road. General Weygands hopes of holding the Somme–Aisne Line were in tatters as he could not stop the German advance. In a series of pincer movements, the Germans cut off and trapped large groups of French troops. Clearly then, Paris could not be protected. Thousands of refugees fled south and west.

On June 10, the French moved their seat of government from Paris to the southern city of Bordeaux. Paris was declared an open city—one that could not be defended. The Germans entered Paris unopposed on June 14. French resistance was crumbling.

THE STUKA DIVE-BOMBER

These Stuka dive bombers helped the Germans conquer numerous European countries in the Blitzkrieg of 1939–1940.

The Stuka was designed to give close support to ground troops. This bomber was a key ingredient in German Blitzkrieg warfare, especially in 1939 and 1940.

Officially designated the Junkers Ju 87, the Stuka entered service in 1937. The Spanish Civil War provided a laboratory for combat testing. The aircraft performed well and was put into full production. Its value was seemingly confirmed by Germany's early-war victories. The Stuka dived down toward its target and dropped bombs with pinpoint accuracy. When it dived, devices on the underside of the aircraft emitted a high-pitched scream designed to create fear and panic.

However, the Stuka's capabilities were overrated. It was slow and had poor defensive armament. It made an easy target for enemy fighters. To operate safely, it needed the Luftwaffe's fighters to control the airspace. When this did not happen, the Stukas suffered heavy losses.

Stukas served throughout the war, but their terrorizing effect was lessened after the heavy losses they took in the Battle of Britain. However, they were modified for a new role. Especially on the eastern front, Stukas mounted heavy cannon that could penetrate tank armor.

Italy's Failed Attacks

As the Germans pressed toward Paris, Italian dictator Benito Mussolini declared war on Britain and France on June 10, 1940. The decision was a reversal of Italian foreign policy. Mussolini was fascinated by Hitler's successes. Italy, he believed, needed military triumphs to boost its reputation. But Italy's army was poorly equipped. The navy was short of fuel and lacked modern aircraft. Italy's industry was short of many key raw materials.

Still, Italy invaded France on July 20, just five days before France surrendered to the Germans. Some 450,000 Italian troops crossed into France. Although they had to fight through mountain passes, the faced just 185,000 French troops. But the defenders stopped the Italians in their tracks. The Italians gained only a few miles in five days. The campaign that Mussolini had expected to boost Italy's reputation ended in humiliation. French losses were only thirty-seven killed, forty-two wounded, and 150 missing.

French Humiliation at Compiègne

By mid-June, France was barely able to continue to fight. Winston Churchill, the British prime minister, feared that the Germans would capture the powerful French fleet. He urged the French to fight on. Some senior French officers, including Charles de Gaulle, also wanted to keep fighting. But others believed that France was only days from total defeat. On June 16, 1940, Prime Minister Reynaud, who wanted to continue fighting, resigned. His replacement was in favor of an immediate stop to fighting. He and others argued for an immediate armistice, or end of hostilities, in order to save lives and arrange better terms with the Germans.

Some senior French officers, including Charles de Gaulle, also wanted to keep fighting. But others believed that France was only days from total defeat.

On June 16 the French government sought an armistice. De Gaulle boarded an aircraft for England, determined to continue the fight. His supporters became known as the Free French.

VICHY AND THE FREE FRENCH

When France surrendered, a new government was set up in the southern half of France. The seat of government was at the resort town of Vichy. This smaller country was independent, at least in theory. The Germans occupied the northern half of the country, as well as the entire Atlantic coast. The French army was disarmed and sent home. The French fleet became a source of concern for the British government over the following months.

Vichy France's relationship with Nazi Germany remains controversial. Some French politicians had Nazi beliefs. Others simply hoped to preserve France in some semi-independent form. Still, the Germans treated Vichy ruthlessly. They exploited the country's economic resources for the benefit of Germany. Some 800,000 French workers were encouraged or forced to work in German industry. The Vichy government also cooperated in actions against the country's Jewish citizens.

Opposition to Vichy France and the Nazis centered on the Free French movement. Its leader was Charles de Gaulle, in exile in Britain. As the Nazi occupation wore on, more and more ordinary French people rejected the Vichy regime and fought back. They formed the French Resistance. The Allies supported them with supplies, and they played a key role in the fight against the Nazis. Regular Free French units also served with the Allied armies and fought in many of the major battles later in the war.

Armistice negotiations began on June 21. They were held in the town of Compiègne. In a gesture of revenge, the Germans held the negotiations in the same railroad car that had been used at the end of World War I. The Germans presented a document of twenty-four articles and demanded that they be accepted. The French could do little but agree. The French representative, General Charles Huntziger, signed the document on June 25. He was then flown to Rome to sign a similar agreement with Mussolini.

The end of the fighting marked the end of an amazing period in the history of warfare. Using the doctrine of Blitzkrieg, Hitler had conquered much of Europe in six weeks, at very little cost. Only Britain remained unconquered. And Britain was greatly weakened.

▶ German bombs caused much destruction in England during the Battle of Britain.

2 The Isolation of Britain

KEY PEOPLE	KEY PLACES	
🇬🇧 Winston Churchill	🇬🇧 London, England	🏴 Mers-el-Kébir, French North Africa
🇫🇷 Charles de Gaulle	🇫🇷 Toulon, France	
卐 Rudolph Hess		卐 Berlin, Germany

For the eighteen months between June 1940 and December 1941, the British stood alone against the might of Nazi Germany. Nearly every other European country had been defeated, supported the Germans, or refused to choose sides.

Britain's leader, Winston Churchill, prepared his people for the threat of a Nazi invasion. With limited resources at hand, Churchill also worked hard to win the support of new allies, including the United States.

Britain Alone

The total defeat of France in June 1940 left Adolf Hitler in control of western Europe. Only Britain opposed him. Britain was in a dangerous position. Germany was victorious and powerful. The Germans were poised to launch an invasion of southeast England from northern France. The English Channel, barely 20 miles (32 km) wide, seemed to offer little protection. Many in Britain wanted to make peace with Germany. Others rejected the idea of compromising. The new prime minister, Winston Churchill, embodied this spirit of resistance.

In a radio address on June 18, Churchill summed up the current military and political situation: "What General Weygand called the Battle of France is over. I expect the Battle of Britain is about to begin. Upon this battle depends the survival of Christian civilization. Upon it depends our own British life, and the long continuity of our institutions and our empire. The whole fury and might of the enemy must very soon be turned upon us. Hitler knows that he will have to break us in this island or lose the war. Let us therefore brace ourselves to our duties, and so bear ourselves that, if the British Empire and its Commonwealth last for a thousand years, men will still say: 'This was their finest hour.'"

Although Churchill's speeches were inspiring, Britain had few resources for fighting. The British army had managed to escape from Dunkirk, but it was in a poor state. Many units were recovering from the evacuation. The rest were made up of new, untrained recruits. Most of the army's heavy equipment such as tanks had been left behind at Dunkirk.

Britain worked furiously to rebuild and strengthen her defenses. Weapons factories boosted their output. U. S. president Franklin D. Roosevelt decided to allow Britain to buy 500,000 rifles and 900 artillery pieces on a "cash and carry" basis. The British people were ready to fight, even though the situation seemed grim. Volunteers flocked to the new civil defense force, called the Home Guard. It was mostly made up of men too young or too old to serve in the regular army. By August 1940, 1 million men had joined. Yet, they still faced a much larger German army.

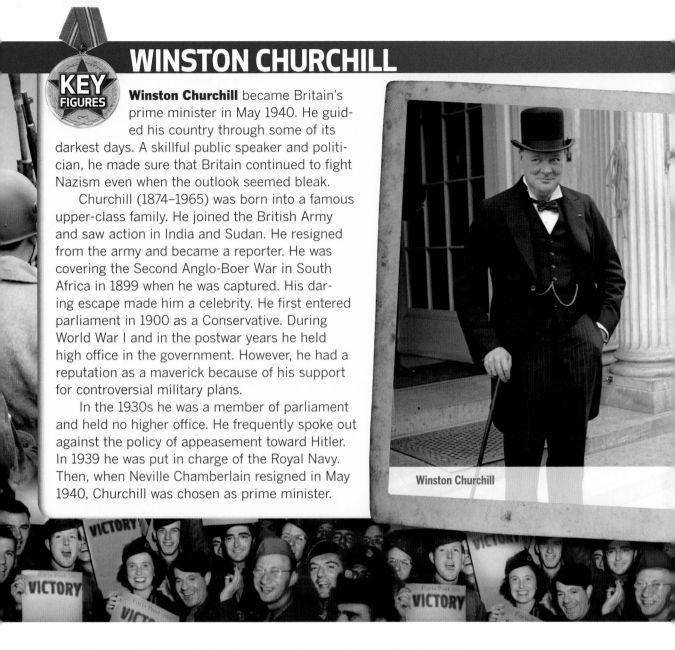

WINSTON CHURCHILL

Winston Churchill became Britain's prime minister in May 1940. He guided his country through some of its darkest days. A skillful public speaker and politician, he made sure that Britain continued to fight Nazism even when the outlook seemed bleak.

Churchill (1874–1965) was born into a famous upper-class family. He joined the British Army and saw action in India and Sudan. He resigned from the army and became a reporter. He was covering the Second Anglo-Boer War in South Africa in 1899 when he was captured. His daring escape made him a celebrity. He first entered parliament in 1900 as a Conservative. During World War I and in the postwar years he held high office in the government. However, he had a reputation as a maverick because of his support for controversial military plans.

In the 1930s he was a member of parliament and held no higher office. He frequently spoke out against the policy of appeasement toward Hitler. In 1939 he was put in charge of the Royal Navy. Then, when Neville Chamberlain resigned in May 1940, Churchill was chosen as prime minister.

Winston Churchill

The Royal Navy had taken some losses during the Dunkirk evacuation, but remained powerful. The naval bases in the far north of Scotland remained intact. But British leaders were worried. If the Germans tried to invade, the British high command thought the German's land-based aircraft as well as German U-boats (submarines) might swamp the British navy in the narrow waters of the English Channel.

Britain was also protected by the fighter squadrons of the Royal Air Force (RAF). On paper, Britain seemed to be at a disadvantage against the Luftwaffe. British losses in France had been high. Although aircraft production had been increased dramatically, the RAF had just 620 fighters. The Luftwaffe had 1,200 fighters and 1,300 bombers available. The RAF also had a shortage of trained pilots. However, experienced pilots from Czechoslovakia and Poland were joining the RAF. Other pilots from throughout the British Empire joined as well. And volunteers from many other countries joined. Many of these came from the United States. They formed the "Eagle Squadrons." But even with these additions, the RAF was badly outnumbered.

> *They formed the "Eagle Squadrons." But even with these additions, the RAF was badly outnumbered.*

However, the British did have several advantages. First, Britain had a network of radar sites along the coast. These radar sites let them detect incoming German aircraft and respond. Second, the RAF was fighting over friendly territory. The Germans would be operating far from their bases. German fighters could not remain over Britain for long without running short of fuel. Also, any German pilots who were shot down over England and survived would become prisoners. Their British equivalents could fight another day.

> *Over the months that followed, Britain teetered on the brink of defeat. Yet Churchill remained defiant.*

Over the months that followed, Britain teetered on the brink of defeat. Yet Churchill remained defiant. His speeches stressed the evils of Nazism and the need to protect democracy. These messages were directed both toward the British people and the United States. Churchill needed strong allies. Hitler assisted him in 1941, first by invading the Soviet Union and then by declaring war on the United States.

Although Churchill generally worked well with President Franklin D. Roosevelt, he distrusted Joseph Stalin. Like Roosevelt, Churchill was concerned about Stalin's ambitions and intentions for the postwar world.

Churchill also had disagreements with senior U.S. military leaders. Roosevelt had agreed to a "Europe-first" strategy. However, many of Roosevelt's generals thought that Japan should be the priority. The leaders also argued over where and when the Allies should invade in Axis-occupied Europe. The first joint U.S.-British operation was in North Africa in November 1942. This operation was followed by invasions of Sicily and the Italian mainland. These choices reflected Churchill's wishes. He preferred to attack Germany indirectly by striking its weaker ally, Italy. Most U.S. commanders favored an all-out invasion of northwest Europe. This disagreement was resolved in 1943, when plans were made for the invasion of France in 1944.

Most U.S. commanders favored an all-out invasion of northwest Europe.

During the time when the invasion plans were being settled, Roosevelt and Churchill had a close relationship. In the conferences between the Allies, Churchill gradually became the junior partner in the Allied leadership. His country was worn out with fighting. Britain also could not match the financial and military resources of the new superpowers. As a result of his declining popularity and despite his wartime service, Churchill was voted out of office in 1945. Britain turned away from the wartime hero to concentrate on reforms. Churchill did serve again as prime minister again in the 1950s, but he was ill and out of tune with the prevailing mood. Nevertheless, he was still popular and highly regarded. At his death, the nation mourned their loss of Winston Churchill.

This British postage stamp commemorates Winston Churchill.

German Plans for Invasion

Germany had been planning for an invasion of Britain since before the fall of France. The head of the German navy, Grand Admiral Erich Raeder, ordered his staff to draw up proposals for an invasion. At first, these discussions did not win much response from Hitler. He had hoped that Britain might agree to an offer of a peaceful settlement. By July, however, Hitler was considering an invasion, which was given the code name Sealion.

This map of Operation Sealion shows the German plan to invade England. It was never carried out.

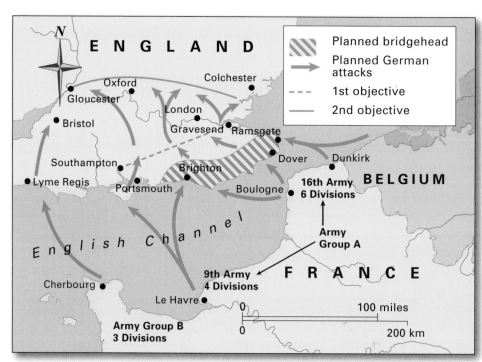

On July 19 Churchill rejected Hitler's offer of peaceful settlement. Eight days later, the commander of the German army presented Hitler with formal plans for Operation Sealion. In this plan, forty-one tank and infantry divisions, along with two airborne divisions, would cross the English Channel on or just after August 25.

Grand Admiral Raeder immediately protested. The German navy did not have the transport ships to move that many troops. He also could not defend such a large invasion fleet without absolute control of the air. The army presented a new plan for a smaller invasion with twenty-seven divisions, and postponed the operation until September 21 to allow Raeder to gather support. But everyone agreed that the Luftwaffe had to destroy the RAF before the invasion could begin.

The Luftwaffe had been trying to draw the British into air battles by bombing ships and ports along England's south coast. But the RAF held back most of its strength. On August 1 Hitler issued new orders. The Luftwaffe was to smash the RAF as quickly as possible.

The Battle of Britain

The Luftwaffe's mission was to destroy all RAF's aircraft, radar network, and airfields. So they began with direct attacks on these targets. Initially the RAF did well. But as the Germans continued to attack almost every day, they started to grind down the RAF. Between August 24 and September 6, 1940, the RAF lost 282 aircraft, mostly fighters. The Luftwaffe lost 378 bombers and fighters in that period. But the Luftwaffe's greater numbers meant things were going in their favor. Between fifteen and twenty British pilots were killed and wounded each day. Pilots still available were increasingly exhausted. In early September, it seemed that a German invasion was likely to happen.

Events shifted in favor of the RAF on September 7. On that day, German aircraft bombed London in revenge for a British raid on Berlin. The raids on London, known as the Blitz, pounded the city for fifty-seven days. But the Luftwaffe did not have nearly enough planes to attack the RAF and London at the same time.

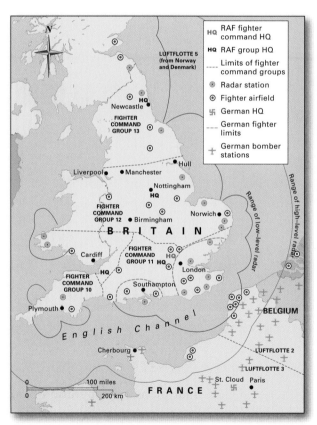

As Germany planned its attack on the RAF, it targeted the RAF's aircraft, radar network, and airfields.

BRITAIN'S RADAR DEFENSES

TECH

The British had a key advantage over the Germans in the Battle of Britain: radar stations that dotted the coast. These stations told the British the number, height, and direction of attacking German aircraft.

This early-warning system of fifty-one radar sites was built just before the war, between 1937 and 1939. The sites were mainly along the eastern and southern coasts. The radar could find approaching aircraft from 50 to 120 miles (80 to 192 km) away. Britain's air defense system also included ground observers, antiaircraft artillery, and the fighter planes of the RAF. Information was gathered and sent to RAF Fighter Command's headquarters outside London.

As German planes approached, fighter squadrons would "scramble" to meet the attacking aircraft. Speed was important, as the British fighters had to take off, gain altitude, and fly to the enemy within minutes of the danger first being detected. The Luftwaffe attacked the radar stations, but the system proved durable. Radar continued to play an important role in the rest of World War II. New developments made it more and more effective as a military tool.

The Blitz gave the RAF time to make up its losses and repair its airfield. As the RAF recovered, they shot down more and more German planes.

The Blitz gave the RAF time to make up its losses and repair its airfields. As the RAF recovered, they shot down more and more German planes. Between September 7 and 30, the Germans lost 380 aircraft; the RAF lost 178 aircraft. German attacks continued, but they became smaller and less frequent.

Hitler Turns to the East

As the Battle of Britain turned against Germany, Operation Sealion became less likely. By October it was clear that the Luftwaffe was not going to beat the RAF. On October 12 the invasion was officially postponed "indefinitely." In reality, it had been abandoned.

Hitler had already turned his attention elsewhere—to war against the Soviet Union. Hitler considered the Communist USSR to be the great ideological enemy of Nazism. In late 1940, most German forces began leaving France and moving east. The invasion threat to Britain was over. From this point on, it would be up to the German navy, particularly its U-boats, to wage war against Britain. They would try to cripple Britain's economy.

Beginning the invasion of the Soviet Union, code-named Barbarossa, while Britain remained undefeated, meant that Germany waged a dangerous war on two fronts. Several top German generals warned Hitler of this mistake, but his mind was made up to combat a fiercer enemy.

Hess's Bizarre Mission

Hitler still hoped for peace with Britain. He probably discussed this desire with other top Nazi officials. Whatever the case, this led to one of the strangest episodes of the war. In May 1941 Rudolph Hess, the deputy leader of the Nazi Party, flew alone from Germany and crash landed in Scotland. Hess stated he was seeking peace, but British authorities dismissed his claims and put him in prison. On hearing the news, Hitler stripped Hess of his position and declared him insane.

The story of Hess's puzzling mission has been studied ever since it happened. Many questions remain unanswered.

One of Hitler's top assistants, Rudolph Hess, flew to Britain in 1941 in an apparent attempt to make peace. After his trial and conviction at Nuremberg, he spent the rest of his life in a German prison. He died in 1987 at the age of ninety-one.

Attacks on Vichy France

One of Churchill's key concerns in the summer of 1940 was the allegiance of Vichy France. Vichy France's large fleet was concentrated in ports of the Mediterranean and West Africa. Vichy officials stated that their ships would remain neutral. Still, Churchill, worried the fleet would fall into German hands. He decided to eliminate this threat.

Early on July 3, French ships anchored in British harbors were captured by force. That afternoon, a British fleet appeared outside the French naval base at Mers-el-Kébir on the Moroccan coast. The Vichy French faced the choice of surrendering their ships, sinking them deliberately, or attacking the British. Negotiations dragged on, and the British opened fire in the late afternoon. They sank one French battleship and damaged two others. However, several Vichy warships survived. The British attacked again, this time with carrier-borne aircraft. Still, some Vichy warships managed to escape and regrouped at Toulon on the south coast of France.

They sank one French battleship and damaged two others.

The British, along with Free French forces under Charles de Gaulle, also attacked the Vichy French naval base at Dakar on the West African coast. However, the Vichy French forces drove back the attack. Churchill ordered a halt to the attack. Churchill's decisions undermined Britain's prestige and ultimately soured relations between Churchill and de Gaulle.

Britain's Commando Raids

After mostly removing the threat of the Vichy fleet, the British also conducted large operations in the Mediterranean and Middle East during 1940–1941. These campaigns were important, but they did not greatly weaken Germany's war machine. Britain did not have the military strength fully to challenge Nazi power in Europe. Still, Churchill wanted to take the fight to Europe. Doing so would boost the morale of the British people and those in Nazi-occupied countries. The RAF's bombers were conducting raids, but these were little more than pinpricks. Churchill wanted some offensive action by ground forces. His demands led to raids by new units of elite troops known as commandos.

Their attacks in 1940 were small. Their raids in the following year were more significant. Two raids struck against targets in Norway. They destroyed German-controlled plants that made ingredients for explosives. These raids also made Hitler suspect that Norway was a weak link. He diverted 372,000 German troops to defend Norway. However, these troops would have been much more useful in other war zones in Europe.

Churchill's Search for Aid and Allies

Britain was effectively alone in 1940–1941, but it could draw on Australia, Canada, India, New Zealand, and other colonies for troops and resources. Also, Britain was a refuge for many European governments-in-exile, but these allies were insufficient to challenge Hitler's domination of Europe.

The ally that Churchill most desired during this period was the United States. Isolationism was strong among the U.S. public, but President Franklin D. Roosevelt was sympathetic to the British. Churchill's speeches, which often spoke of defending freedom and democracy from tyranny, were written in part to win the support of the U.S. public.

President Roosevelt could not commit his country to war. But he stretched the limits of neutrality. He announced a "destroyers for bases" deal with Britain in 1940 and the Lend-Lease Bill in March 1941. These provided the British with weapons to continue the war effort.

Operation Barbarossa, the German invasion of the Soviet Union in June 1941, gave Britain its first new ally. However, the Soviet Union was far away and distrusted by some. In the early part of the war, the alliance was militarily weak and lacked coordination. From the beginning of Barbarossa to the end of 1942, the Soviet Union was barely able to survive. Britain, struggling to rearm and expand its armed forces, could offer only limited support by sending convoys to the Soviet Union through arctic waters.

The United States finally joined the Allies after the Japanese attack on Pearl Harbor on December 7, 1941. Four days later Germany and Italy declared war on the United States in support of their Axis partner. British and U.S. leaders met in late December, 1941. They decided to focus on Germany first and agreed to share the planning of their military operations.

▶British Matilda tanks of the 4th Royal Tank regiment in North Africa.

3 The Mediterranean, Africa, and the Middle East, 1940 to 1941

KEY PEOPLE	KEY PLACES	
General Claude Auchinleck	Alexandria, Egypt	Tobruk, Libya
Marshal Rodolfo Graziani	Gibraltar	Malta
Field Marshal Erwin Rommel	Taranto, Italy	Suez Canal
Major General Richard O'Connor		
General Archibald Wavell		

Control of the Mediterranean was vital to Britain at the start of World War II. The Mediterranean and the Suez Canal formed the shortest sea link to the most important colonies of the British Empire: Australia, India, New Zealand, and the large naval base at Singapore. The loss of the Suez Canal would mean that ships would have to travel the much longer route around the southern tip of Africa.

To protect the canal, the British stationed a major force of troops and ships in Egypt. Britain's main base in the eastern Mediterranean was Alexandria, Egypt. The island of Malta was the main base in the central Mediterranean. To the west, Gibraltar was another key British base. It guarded the passage from the Atlantic to the Mediterranean.

By mid-1940, after the fall of France, Britain's position in the region was weak. It seemed possible that the Spanish Fascist dictator Francisco Franco might side with Germany. Hitler had aided Franco in the Spanish Civil war. Spain might attack Gibraltar, or allow German forces to move through Spain to accomplish the same task. In reality, Franco had no intention of allowing Spain to become involved in a full-blown world war.

There were also questions over Vichy French-controlled territories, where sizeable naval and army forces were present. It was not clear whether these would be neutral or side with Germany. The French colonies of Algeria, Morocco, and Tunisia dominated North Africa. Another French colony, Syria, in the eastern Mediterranean, might also become a threat to the Suez Canal.

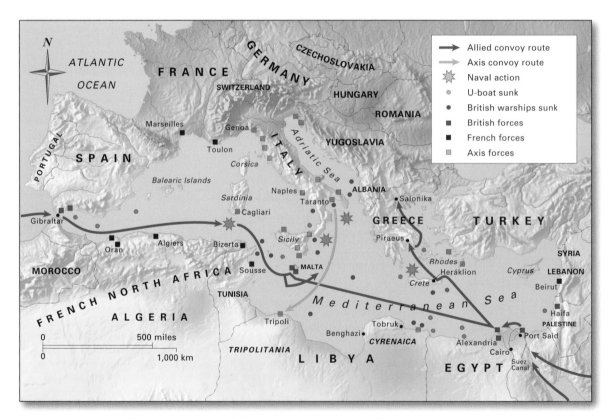

This map shows the main battles on land and sea in the Mediterranean from 1940 to 1941.

Italy's North African Offensive

The greatest threat in 1940 was posed by Italy, which had a large, modern fleet and a number of colonies in Africa. Chief among these were Libya and Italian Somaliland. Italian dictator Benito Mussolini also realized that the British base on Malta threatened his links across the Mediterranean to Libya. His goal was to push Britain out of the Mediterranean. He ordered Italian troops in Libya and Italian Somaliland to invade Egypt. He planned to bomb or starve Malta until it surrendered. He also planned to invade Greece, which would give Italy control of the northern Mediterranean.

Mussolini . . .planned to bomb or starve Malta until it surrendered. He also planned to invade Greece, which would give Italy control of the northern Mediterranean.

On paper, the British seemed quite weak. General Archibald Wavell commanded 36,000 troops in Egypt, 27,000 in Palestine, and much smaller numbers of troops in other colonies. The British had only a few aircraft, and most were outdated. The Mediterranean Fleet was strong, but it would have to operate in small waters. Also it would face the whole of the Italian navy, and would have to operate within range of land-based Italian aircraft.

Mussolini had 200,000 troops based in Libya, commanded by Marshal Rodolfo Graziani. Another 110,000 troops were stationed in the African colonies of Abyssinia (now Ethiopia), Eritrea, and Italian Somaliland. These Italian troops would march against a much smaller British force.

On September 13, 1940, the Italians struck against Egypt. Five divisions advanced along the coastline of the Mediterranean. Small British detachments guarding the border fell back from the overwhelming Italian force. Control of the Suez Canal seemed within Graziani's grasp. But Graziani did not seize the opportunity to press forward. After advancing 50 miles (80 km) to reach Sidi Barrani, he ordered his units to build fortifications. The main British force, some two divisions, was based 75 miles (120 km) east. For the next several weeks the Italians strengthened defenses.

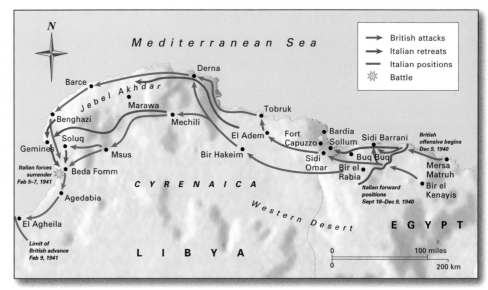

The British counter-offensive (December 1940 to February 1941). Marshal Graziani, the Italian commander, led 200,000 troops against a much weaker British force. After months of stalemate the Italians were pushed back into Libya.

Wavell's Counterattack

General Wavell intended to push the Italians out of Egypt. The operation began on December 9, 1940. The British forces, including 275 tanks, launched its own Blitzkrieg-style attack against the Italian forts. British aircraft and warships joined in the attack, blasting the enemy's positions. The Italians were no match for the fast-moving British attacks. Whole units were cut off and surrendered. Within days, 40,000 Italians had given up. The remnants of the Italian invasion force retreated back to Bardia, Libya.

Wavell sensed the opportunity for further gains. He resumed his attack at the end of December. The British quickly captured Bardia and pushed deeper into Libya. They captured the port of Tobruk on January 22. The Italian forces fell apart and retreated along the coast. Moving quickly across the interior, the British 7th Armored Division reached the town of Beda Fomm just thirty minutes before the retreating Italians. The Italian forces were cut off. Two days later they surrendered.

For the loss of fewer than 2,000 men, the British had captured 130,000 enemy troops. The victory was inspirational and boosted British morale. But many of Wavell's troops were quickly sent to Greece. Their departure left only a few scattered British units to hold onto the newly won positions in Libya.

East Africa and the Mediterranean

The British suffered setbacks in East Africa in 1940. In August, Italian troops from Abyssinia attacked and captured two key ports, Berbera and Djibouti. Control of these two ports would allow the Italians to close the southern entrance to the Red Sea and the Suez Canal. After an initial defeat, the British began to push the Italians out of East Africa. At the same time, Britain's Royal Navy scored several victories against the Italian navy in the Mediterranean. The most important of these was a surprise attack on the Italian naval base of Taranto.

In August, Italian troops from Abyssinia attacked and captured two key ports, Berbera and Djibouti. Control of these two ports would allow the Italians to close the southern entrance to the Red Sea and the Suez Canal.

TARANTO

KEY EVENTS

On the night of November 11, 1940, a group of twenty-one British Swordfish biplanes took off from the aircraft carrier *Illustrious*. They flew 150 miles (240 km) to Taranto harbor in southern Italy. Using torpedoes, the outdated airplanes crippled the Italian fleet. They sank three enemy battleships and damaged two cruisers. Two of the torpedo bombers were shot down.

The attack left just one Italian battleship fit for action. This gave the British a key advantage in the region. The Italian fleet was no longer willing to fight the Royal Navy head-to-head. The raid on Taranto was closely studied by the Japanese. They used it as a blueprint for their larger attack on the U.S. naval base at Pearl Harbor in December 1941.

DESERT WAR

STRATEGY & TACTICS

The back-and-forth nature of the North African campaign was partly due to the geography of the region. The terrain placed certain limitations on the commanders of both sides. Most of the fighting took place along a narrow coastal strip. An east-west road, the only decent road, crossed the coastal strip. The main towns in the region were strung out along the road. The desert interior was mostly empty with a few wells and poor quality tracks. In many places, vehicles could not pass through it.

Although North Africa could host many tanks, it was an unpleasant place to fight for the ordinary soldier. Extreme hot and cold, sandstorms, and flies all made life difficult.

Another problem was the size of the battle area. Opposing armies could advance or retreat hundreds of miles. The distance created problems in resupplying the armies, particularly with fuel and water. These supplies had to be transported from bases hundreds of miles away. Therefore, the capture or defense of ports near the front line, such as Tobruk, was important to both sides.

Because of the geography, commanders generally could choose to advance along the coast road. The road would make passage easier, but the enemy would be defending fortifications and settlements. As an alternative, the attacking forces could launch an advance through the desert interior. Then they could hit their enemy in the side or rear. Both sides tried both approaches.

Finally, the Desert War was fought with relatively small forces. Both sides needed to send troops to other areas. By late 1942 the Germans had more urgent priorities, especially fighting in Russia. At the same time, the entry of the United States into the war in late 1941 greatly assisted British troops.

The Italian Collapse in East Africa

By early 1941, the British seemed to be in a stronger position in the Mediterranean and the Middle East. But there were still many potential threats. General Wavell made a plan to attack the Italian colonies in East Africa. A force of 28,000, including Indian and Free French troops, attacked eastward from the British colony of Sudan. In a series of battles, the Italians were forced back. The Italian troops fought stubbornly, but finally surrendered on April 8.

British Crisis in the Mediterranean

The British experienced success in East Africa in 1941. At the same time, the situation in the Mediterranean grew worse. The British base at Malta was the key to controlling the central Mediterranean. But Malta was within range of Axis aircraft based in Italy. The Italians launched some bombing attacks in 1940. In 1941, Germany sent air units to join in the attacks against the British base in Malta.

The Italians launched some bombing attacks in 1940. In 1941, Germany sent air units to join in the attacks against the British base in Malta.

In January 1941, German dive-bombers damaged the British aircraft carrier *Illustrious* and sunk the cruiser *Southampton*. The Luftwaffe then concentrated on Malta, inflicting heavy losses. By mid-March the defenders on Malta were down to just eight fighter aircraft. The German attacks grew more and more frequent and damaging. Just as Malta seemed ripe to fall, Hitler ordered the Luftwaffe to shift to the war in the Balkans and in North Africa.

This helped the British rebuild their forces in Malta. They went back on the attack, using aircraft and submarines to hit Axis supply ships. By late November the British were sinking more than half of the Axis equipment and fuel headed for North Africa. But the German air force and submarines were also waging a fierce war against British shipping. Malta continued to be a major focus of fighting in 1942.

The performance of the Italian navy grew worse. On March 26, a strong Italian fleet set out to attack British ships transporting troops. The British were warned of the Italians' plan. British warships met the Italian fleet at Cape Matapan. They sunk and damaged several major Italian ships. In the battle, the British lost one aircraft and suffered slight damage to one British ship. This defeat crushed the Italians. So they kept their surface fleet out of the fighting for the rest of the war.

Soon after, the Germans inflicted heavy losses on the Royal Navy operating in the Mediterranean. The Germans attacked as forces left the mainland of Greece and Crete. In addition to hitting supply convoys, the Germans also sank the aircraft carrier *Ark Royal* in November, 1941, and the battleship *Barham* in December. Also in December, Italian midget submarines passed quietly into Alexandria harbor. They planted special explosives on two battleships, *Queen Elizabeth* and *Valiant*. The blasts damaged both ships and kept them out of action for several months.

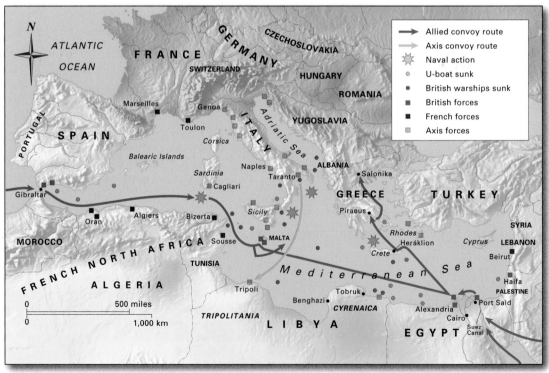

This map shows the Allied and Axis convoy routes and major battles in the Mediterranean (1940 to 1941).

Rommel and the Afrika Korps

The poor showing of the Italians in North Africa, the Mediterranean, and the Balkans embarrassed Mussolini. He dismissed his local commander, Graziani, in February 1941. However, by that time Hitler had taken an interest in North Africa. Hitler sent fighters and bombers to Sicily. Most importantly, he sent a new force to the theater: General Erwin Rommel's Afrika Korps.

Rommel arrived in Libya in February 1941. His orders were to defend Tripoli. Rommel's forces were small, and the Germans believed the British had a vastly superior force. Nevertheless, Rommel attacked immediately. The Afrika Korps and the Italians drove the British back. As the British troops retreated, the Italians advanced along the coast road. At the same time, the German 21st Armored Division raced through the desert. Their target was the port of Tobruk.

"There will be no Dunkirk here. If we should have to get out, we shall have to fight our way out. No surrender and no retreat."

Tobruk was an important prize. Its port facilities allowed equipment and supplies to be unloaded. The British were caught off balance by the speed of the Axis advance. The British 2nd Armored Division, along with Major General Richard O'Connor, were cut off and subsequently captured. The Australian 9th Division was able to reach Tobruk. They hurried to improve the port's defenses as the Axis offensive rolled closer and closer.

Tobruk's defenses consisted of a long antitank ditch and numerous strong points. There were 36,000 British troops manning the defenses. Major General Leslie Morshead of the 9th Australian Division was in command. He made his intentions clear: "There will be no Dunkirk here. If we should have to get out, we shall have to fight our way out. No surrender and no retreat." Rommel's first attacks in April 1941 failed, and losses on both sides were heavy. The Germans settled down and began to pound the defenders with heavy air and artillery attacks. Meanwhile, Italian troops were left to guard Libya's border with Egypt to the east.

ERWIN ROMMEL

Erwin Rommel

Erwin Rommel (1891–1944)

was perhaps the most outstanding German field commander of World War II. He was a master of tank warfare. He was famous in his own country and also admired by his enemies for his skill.

Rommel was a veteran of World War I. At the start of World War II, he was promoted to Hitler's personal headquarters. He led the 7th Armored Division in the defeat of France in 1940. In 1941 he took command of German forces in North Africa. There Rommel earned a reputation as a genius of fast-moving armored warfare. The British nicknamed him the "Desert Fox." His victories in battles also made him a favorite of Hitler. He was promoted to the rank of field marshal after the battle of Tobruk in 1942.

Despite bouts of illness and a military defeat in North Africa in 1943, Rommel became commander of German forces in France in January 1944. He supervised the building of defenses along the coast of France.

On July 17, 1944, shortly after the Allied D-Day landings, Rommel was badly wounded when his car was strafed, or shot up, by a British fighter. While he was recovering, Rommel was implicated in a plot to kill Hitler. Rommel was forced to commit suicide on October 14, 1944 to prevent the mistreatment of his family.

VICTORY

Tobruk and British Relief Efforts

Wavell believed that Rommel's forces were short of supplies. In May and June he launched a series of attacks from Egypt. The goal was to break through to the surrounded forces in Tobruk. The British easily pushed aside the Italians in their path. But then the British came up against Rommel's German forces. Anti-tank guns, including numerous 88-mm guns fir-

...then the British came up against Rommel's German forces.

ing from hidden defensive positions, knocked out most of the British tanks. Then Rommel sent in his own armored divisions. The British had to withdraw to keep from being outflanked. Wavell had been outwitted and defeated. General Claude Auchinleck replaced Wavell as commander on July 1.

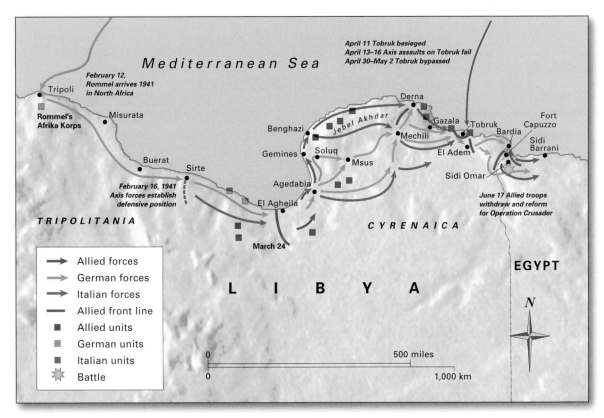

The Battle of Tobruk, 1941. After many months, the British finally achieved success when Rommel retreated.

In November 1941 Auchinleck launched Operation Crusader to relieve Tobruk. Infantry units advanced slowly westward along the coast road. British armor made a sweeping movement through the desert, driving toward Tobruk. Rommel unleashed his panzers and inflicted heavy losses on the British around Sidi Razegh. By June 23 the British had lost some 85 percent of their tanks. The Germans had only ninety tanks left out of 320. But the British had more armored units in reserve, and Rommel did not. In a bold move, Rommel sent his remaining tanks toward the Egyptian border. He hoped the British would pull back to cover the new danger. Auchinleck, however, continued the attack toward Tobruk. This decision proved correct. On November 27, British troops reached Tobruk. At the same time, the German advance ran out of fuel and had to turn back.

THE GERMAN "88"

TECH

One of the most effective and feared weapons of the war, the German Flak Model 18 88-mm gun could destroy the heaviest tanks at long range.

The "88" of the name referred to the diameter of the barrel, 88 millimeters. The gun fired a shell at extremely high speed, which made it very accurate. This heavy gun was originally intended as an antiaircraft weapon. It was first used against tanks during the invasion of Poland in 1939 and France in 1940. The Germans quickly realized it could penetrate thick tank armor.

In North Africa, the gun was towed behind a half-track vehicle. It was set up near the front line so that it could knock out British tanks at long range. Rommel would then send his own tanks in a counterattack.

The "88" did have weaknesses. Once towed into place, it took time to set up. Also, the gun stood up high, making it easy to spot if placed out in the open. As the war went on, the gun was mounted on a variety of vehicles. In its different versions, it was used until the end of the war.

HEINZ WERNER SCHMIDT

Born in South Africa to German parents, Schmidt saw service in Poland and East Africa. He was Rommel's personal aide during the desert campaign. He recorded the destruction inflicted on the British in June 1941.

I accompanied Rommel on a personal inspection of the battlefield along the frontier from Halfaya to Sidi Mar. We counted 180 knocked out British tanks, most Mark Is. Some of them were later recovered from the battlefield, repaired, marked with the German cross, and in due course sent into battle against the men who had manned them before. Rommel's victory was largely due to his use of the 88-mm guns, which were primarily designed for antiaircraft work, as antitank weapons. They were very effectively sited as the core of every defensive position.

A few of the enemy were captured. I overheard in passing a conversation between a staff interrogator and a young English tank driver. "In my opinion," said the Englishman, with an unfriendly glance at a nearby 88, "it is unfair to use flak [antiaircraft guns] against our tanks." A German artillery man who was sitting on his haunches nearby, listening to the interpretation, interjected excitedly: "Yes, and I think it most unfair of you to attack with tanks whose armor nothing but an 88 will penetrate."

Extract from Heinz W. Schmidt's *With Rommel in the Desert*, 1951.

The Germans fell back from Tobruk as well. They set up new defenses further west. Operation Crusader had saved Tobruk and pushed the Germans back. British losses had been heavy, and Rommel's forces still posed a threat. To make matters worse, British and Australian troops were being withdrawn from North Africa and sent to East Asia to fight the Japanese. At the same time, Rommel received reinforcements for a new attack against Egypt.

IRAQ AND SYRIA

By spring 1941, the uncertain political situation in both Iraq and Syria greatly concerned the British, who also feared the spread of German influence in the Middle East. The growing threat to their military operations in the region prompted the British to occupy both countries.

On account of its oil reserves, which were exploited by British companies, Iraq was an important strategic asset and several Royal Air Force bases had been built there during the 1930s with the agreement of the newly independent state. From the beginning of World War II anti-British sentiment was encouraged by a senior Muslim cleric, Amin el Husseini, the Grand Mufti of Jerusalem, and by German agents. On April 1, 1941, a rebellion led by an unhappy politician, Rashid Ali, quickly overthrew the government of Nuri-es-Said and threw out the country's regent, Emir Abdullah Illah.

Rashid appealed to Germany for aid but it was not immediately forthcoming. The Germans had been caught by surprise by the sudden rebellion. In contrast, the British reacted swiftly by landing troops from India close to Basra in southern Iraq during late April. Rashid's response was to lay siege to the RAF base of Habbaniyah, west of Baghdad, and to cut the pipeline from Iraq to Haifa in British-controlled Palestine, thereby endangering the supply of oil to British forces in Egypt. The British replied by pushing troops north from Basra and sending a column into western Iraq from Transjordan.

By late May the British had over-run much of Iraq, and Rashid had fled to neighboring Persia (now Iran). Emir Abdullah was reinstated. However, British units remained to guarantee the safety of his regime and to maintain the flow of oil. The Grand Mufti fled to Germany, where he found favor with the Nazis as their preferred leader of Arab nationalists. He subsequently raised Muslim units in German-occupied countries to fight the Allies.

Syria, a territory mandated to the French at the end of World War I, remained under Vichy control after the defeat of France in 1940. Its location close to Egypt and the Middle East oil fields made it of vital interest to the British, who feared the spread of German influence into the region. German successes in Greece and Crete in April and May 1941 served to increase British concerns. Their worries had already intensified when German aircraft belatedly heading for Iraq were allowed to refuel at Syrian airfields.

British and Free French forces invaded Syria in early June 1941. They advanced from their bases in Palestine and Iraq. The Vichy French garrison, under the command of General Henri Dentz, fought back hard. The fighting took until June 21 for the invaders to capture the city of Damascus, the Syrian capital. Dentz, who had lost over 6,500 men in the fighting, signed a surrender document at Acre on July 14. The Free French took over any abandoned military equipment and 6,000 Vichy French soldiers from the 30,000 who surrendered agreed to join them. Pro-British authorities were then established in Syria and Lebanon for the rest of the war.

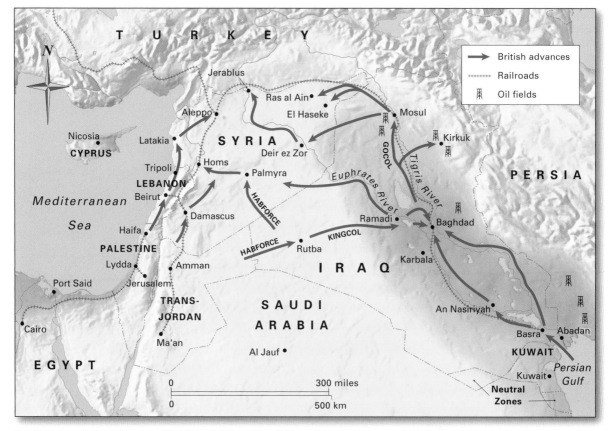

The British used the code names "Habforce," "Kingcol," and "Gocol" for the names of the units involved in military operations in the Middle East in 1940 to 1941. The British were successful in securing the Middle East.

Britain's Desert Generals

North Africa and the Middle East were crucial theaters of war. Prime Minister Winston Churchill wanted the region secured, but he also needed British successes on the battlefield to bolster morale. Consequently, he appointed and dismissed a number of generals, if they did not deliver what Churchill wanted. In August 1942 General Bernard Montgomery resisted political pressures and delayed until he had the forces to defeat the Germans in Egypt. Churchill was furious at the delay. However, Montgomery's tactics gave the prime minister the complete victory that Churchill had demanded from all his desert generals.

▶ The German conquest of Yugoslavia, April 1941.
A Serbian truck burns on the left as German troops pass by.
The German push through Yugoslavia took less than two weeks.

4 The Balkans in Flames

The Balkans, in southern Europe, are a difficult place to wage war. Most of this area is mountainous. The coastline is rugged. Its seas are dotted with hundreds of islands.

The peninsula includes many countries: Yugoslavia, Macedonia, Albania, Bulgaria, Hungary, Romania, and Greece. Each country has its distinct politics and geography. Balkan peoples have warlike traditions. They have a history of defending themselves against invaders.

These obstacles, however, did not stop Italian leader Benito Mussolini from making invasion plans. He wanted to win glory equal to Germany's. Italy had already invaded and occupied Albania. After that, Mussolini wanted to invade Greece and Yugoslavia. But Germany discouraged Italy from trying for more territory. Hitler did not want a war in the Balkans to get in the way of his plans to invade western Europe and the Soviet Union.

Italy's Greek Adventure Fails

Mussolini's first attempt at military glory was in the North African campaigns of 1940. These campaigns were a disaster. The British repelled Italy's invasion into Egypt. More than 150,000 Italian troops were killed, wounded, or captured. Italian colonies, such as Abyssinia (Ethiopia) and Eritrea, were in open revolt. Only when Germany sent troops to North Africa were the Italians saved from total defeat.

Therefore, in late 1940 Mussolini looked for another operation to provide him with a victory. He chose to attack Greece. Italy had little reason to invade Greece. In theory, Greece gave Mussolini a base for attacking British bases in the Mediterranean. But the invasion was basically an attempt to gain military prestige.

On October 28, 1940, 200,000 Italian soldiers invaded Greece from Albania. The Greeks put up a fierce resistance.

Most likely Hitler knew about Mussolini's intentions, and this time he did not object. Hitler felt that British troops would be diverted away from North Africa to defend their ally Greece. Furthermore, it appeared that Italy would easily win a victory. Greece had a small army that was divided along two borders. The Greeks had outdated tanks and broken-down aircraft. Despite these advantages, the Italian forces themselves were unenthusiastic about the war. More importantly, the Greek troops were prepared to defend their homeland.

On October 28, 1940, 200,000 Italian soldiers invaded Greece from Albania. The Greeks put up a fierce resistance. The Italians had to advance through rugged mountains on poor roads. The Greeks used the landscape to their advantage. They inflicted heavy losses on the Italian troops.

Within just two weeks the invasion broke down. The Italians began to retreat, and the Greeks pursued the Italian troops all the way back into Albania. The British Royal Air Force (RAF) arrived to assist the Greeks, taking away the Italian advantage in aircraft. By late December 1940, the Greeks had captured large sections of Albanian territory. Mussolini's bid for glory was a terrible failure.

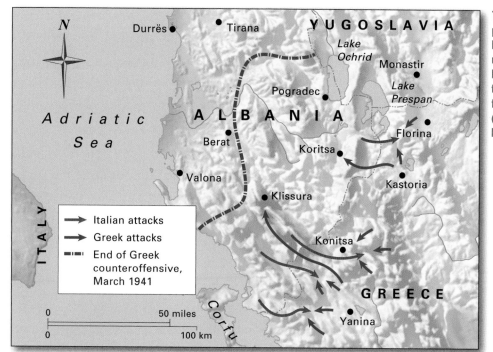

The Greek army pushed the Italians back into Albania using their better knowledge of the terrain and their fierce determination. (October 1940 to March 1941).

Allied and Axis Intervention

Hitler became more and more concerned with events in the Balkans. There were industrial facilities in the Balkans that were important to the German war effort. As the RAF established bases in Greece, they had the range to attack these German targets. Up to 60 percent of Germany's crude oil came from the Romanian oil fields at Ploesti. In addition, much of its lead and nearly all of its tin came from Yugoslavia. Greece and Yugoslavia supplied almost half of Germany's aluminum ore requirements.

Hitler could not allow the Balkans to slip into Allied hands. Many countries in the region were already allied with Germany. This meant that German troops could now march all the way to the Greek border.

The only problem was Yugoslavia. On March 25, 1941, the Yugoslav ruler Prince Paul joined the Axis, angering the people of Yugoslavia. Two days later, two Serbian generals overthrew the prince. In his place they put the seventeen-year-old King Peter II. The generals also tore up the Yugoslavian commitment to the Axis Pact and declared the country's independence. These actions were encouraged by the United States and Britain.

Peter II was eleven years old in 1934 when he became king of Yugoslavia. Prince Paul Karadjordjevic acted as King Peter's regent until the King was seventeen years old. At that time, Prince Paul was ousted by a military coup and King Peter II became the true leader of Yugoslavia.

Hitler was furious. "I have decided to destroy Yugoslavia," Hitler told his senior officers on March 26, 1941.

Meanwhile, British involvement in the Balkans was increasing. The British scored major victories against the Italian fleet in late 1940 and early 1941. The Italian navy began to avoid combat. By January 1941, British troops had landed on Crete and other islands near Greece. In February, a strong force of British troops moved from North Africa to Greece.

In April Hitler launched a German push to conquer the Balkans. It was code-named Operation Marita. A massive force of twenty-four divisions, 1,200 tanks, and a large air force invaded Greece and Yugoslavia.

The Fall of Greece and Yugoslavia

German forces avoided the mistakes the Italians had made. Yugoslavia had a large army—over 1 million soldiers. But the troops were scattered along 1,000 miles (1,609 km) of border. Moreover, the army used horse and mules, in contrast to the Germans armored machines. The Yugoslav air force was made up of old aircraft. It was almost completely destroyed in the first few hours of the invasion by the Luftwaffe. Most importantly, Yugoslavia was politically unstable. The country had been created after World War I. The major territories of Serbia, Croatia, and Slovenia had never been truly united. When the invasion began, Croatia and Slovenia declared independence from Yugoslavia. Many Croatian units even went over to the German side. Civil war flared up and added to the destruction of Yugoslavia.

The Yugoslav air force was made up of old aircraft. It was almost completely destroyed in the first few hours of the invasion by the Luftwaffe.

Under these conditions, the complete collapse of Yugoslavia seemed certain. German bombers pounded the capital city, Belgrade. German troops invaded from several directions. Italian forces pushed toward the coastal cities. As a result, the Yugoslav army was split by the opposing forces and encircled. On April 12 Belgrade was captured. On April 17 the Yugoslav army surrendered.

The German invasion of Greece was also impressive. Most of the Greek and British forces were set up to defend the eastern half of the country. They did not attack the Greek mountain positions. Instead they moved quickly down the mountain valleys and then attacked from the rear. The Germans cut off Greek reinforcements. Also, the Greeks were relying on the resistance of Yugoslavia to protect the northeastern border from a German invasion. But Yugoslavia quickly collapsed, leaving Greece open to attack. The Germans quickly seized the advantage. Before the fighting in Yugoslavia was even over, German forces drove into Greece. They rapidly encircled many Greek and British defenders.

THE BALKANS: HITLER'S FATAL DIVERSION?

Many historians feel that Germany's invasion of the Balkans was Hitler's biggest mistake of World War II. The Balkans were no military threat to Germany prior to the Italian invasion of Greece. Romania, Bulgaria, and Hungary all eventually joined the Axis. Yugoslavia and Greece were content to remain neutral.

Hitler was planning to invade the Soviet Union in May 1941. When the Italian invasion of Greece in April 1941 fell apart, Hitler had to intervene. The German conquest of Yugoslavia and Greece delayed the launch of the invasion into the USSR until June. The delay meant that Hitler was unable to take Moscow before the fall rains turned the roads to mud. The severe winter that followed stopped the German advance. The Soviet military was able to recover and strengthen its defenses. It seems possible that, if Hitler had not been involved in the Balkans, he would have defeated the USSR, and so possibly have won the entire war.

Such arguments, though, are misleading. Hitler could not have invaded the Soviet Union until June, regardless of the Balkans. It took longer than planned to position 3 million German troops, along with thousands of tanks and artillery.

If Mussolini had not failed in the Balkans, Hitler would have been unlikely to invade the region. But once Britain had bases in Greece, RAF planes could attack Germany's sources of supplies. Hitler might have been justified in moving into the Balkans. However, invading the Balkans was just one more operation that stretched German resources to the limit.

The Greek and Allied forces were forced to retreat. German Stuka dive-bombers struck at the weary Allied troops on the roads. A German parachute drop attempted to cut off the retreating forces, but it was too late. By April 27–28 the Allies had reached the coast of Greece. From there they were evacuated by ship to Crete, a large island about 60 miles (100 km) south of the mainland. Some 43,000 British and Commonwealth troops escaped. But most of their heavy military equipment was left behind. Greece had fallen.

In Operation Marita, the German forces pushed into Greece from Yugoslavia in April 1941. When Greece fell to the German advance, the British troops were forced to evacuate from the southern coast to Crete.

The Airborne Battle for Crete

Crete presented a difficult problem for the Germans. By mid-May 1941 the island was heavily defended by 30,000 British and New Zealand troops. They were commanded by Major General Bernard Freyberg. The Allies could use Crete for air strikes against the Germans in the Balkans. If the Germans could capture Crete, they could use it to attack the British in Egypt and Libya. But British warships controlled most of the Mediterranean. A German amphibious invasion of Crete was impossible.

The task was given to German parachute forces. These forces were called Fliegerkorps XI. The Fliegerkorps commander, General Karl Student, drew up the plan for the invasion of Crete. It would involve thousands of troops landing by parachute and glider aircraft. The plan, called Operation Mercury, was very risky, but Hitler finally gave his approval. The scene was set for a unique battle.

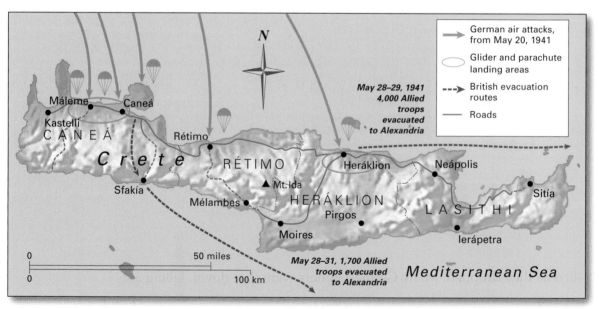

In the German airborne invasion of Crete in May 1941, gliders silently dropped thousands of paratroopers on the island. The Germans lost many men and planes.

ADOLF STRAUCH

Adolf Strauch, a German paratrooper during the Battle of Crete, gave a first-hand account of parachuting into battle.

At about 16:00 hours "Get Ready!" In front of us is the coast of Crete. "Ready to jump!" Our height [from] which we shall drop is 500 feet (150 m). The siren sounds. We jump. I hang in the air and try to orientate myself. I make a good landing in a vineyard. I reach my weapons container. We assemble and take up formation. Enemy reaction is weak. The heat is unbearable. The 1st Regiment flies in in close waves. They, too, jump at 500 feet (150 m) at a speed of 75 mph (120 km/h). There are no German fighter aircraft to be seen. The British antiaircraft artillery and field guns fire continually. Burning machines drop out of the sky. We can see individual Jaeger (riflemen) jumping out of the exits. The pilots hold their machines on course until they crash. A whole battalion has been destroyed. The night is cool. We have dug in, ready to face the enemy who will come from the west.

Extract from *Storming Eagles: German Airborne Forces in World War II*, James Lucas, Cassell & Co., 2001.

Operation Mercury began on May 20, 1941. British and New Zealand troops awoke to the sound of airplane engines. Looking up, they saw thousands of parachutes in the sky. Instantly, the Allies put up a storm of fire. The German paratroopers were defenseless while in the air. Hundreds were killed as they dropped. Many German gliders were shot down, killing all the troops aboard. More than one hundred paratroopers drowned when they landed in the sea. Despite these heavy losses, the Germans gained a foothold on the island.

British code-breaking teams intercepted German transmissions about the invasion. Freyberg knew the Germans' intentions. Yet his troops were not ready. It may be that Freyberg misinterpreted the information. Or, he may not have been allowed to use the information. The British didn't want the Germans to find out that they had broken their secret code.

On the second day of the invasion, the Germans made gains. They captured an airfield, and then defeated a heavy Allied counterattack. Aircraft then landed, bringing in more than 650 fresh German troops. Allied forces started to withdraw to the east and south. The Germans fought their way forward, backed by constant attacks by bombers. The Allies fought hard, but Freyberg realized Crete would be lost. He ordered an evacuation. Around 18,000 Allied troops were successfully taken off by Royal Navy ships. But another 12,000 were unable to escape and became prisoners. Almost 2,000 Allied soldiers were killed.

EYEWITNESS

GERMAN INVADERS ON CRETE

Second Lieutenant Peter Wildey, New Zealand forces, described his initial experience of defending against German invaders on Crete, 1941.

Well, we were having breakfast. We'd just finished it, I think, when all of a sudden two gliders came in. So I opened up my tommy gun. They were at a very low altitude. I had a hundred-round magazine, and I managed to pour the whole lot into those two. I couldn't help hitting some, just raking it from stem to stern. After I got going, the others started joining in. Shortly after that, just right on their heels, these big transports came in. . . The chaps just started pouring out of them. We fired at them as they were coming down, as hard as we could. Others were coming down and they were swinging in the air, from side to side like a pendulum. I think that was a ruse to make it hard to shoot them. I cottoned on, and I waited until the end of the swing and kept my tommy gun pointing there till they came back the next time and I managed to shoot at two or three. Whether I killed them or wounded them, I don't know.

Extract reproduced courtesy of Ministry for Culture and Heritage, New Zealand.

AIR ATTACK AT CORINTH

Prior to the Airborne Attack at Corinth, Germans had used parachute troops in the Balkans. So the massive airborne assault on Crete in May 1941 was not a new tactic. Previously in April, the Allies were in full retreat in Greece. The army was moving toward the southern part of Greece, where the troops might be evacuated to Crete. One escape route was over a bridge across the Corinth Canal in western Greece. If the Germans could capture the bridge, thousands of Allies would be trapped. The Germans could also use the bridge to speed up their advance south.

The German 2nd Parachute Regiment attacked the bridge by glider and paratroopers in the early dawn of April 26. A group of fifty-four paratrooper engineers landed with great accuracy around the bridge. The troops disembarked, overcame the British resistance, and removed the charges that the British had placed on the bridge. The British had actually intended to blow up the bridge if necessary to prevent the Germans from taking it. Although successful at first, the German parachute operation was undone when stray fire hit the explosives that the Germans had removed. An enormous explosion destroyed the bridge and the canal bank.

Other German paratroopers arrived to capture local British antiaircraft and the infantry units. However, their mission was not a success, since the bridge had been destroyed and most of the Allies had already moved south. The Germans lost sixty-three paratroopers. These losses were just a hint of the heavy casualties the Germans would suffer on Crete in May 1941.

For the Germans, Operation Mercury was a success, but the price was very high. More than 7,000 paratroopers, about one-third of the airborne forces used on Crete, were killed or wounded. These losses were so high that the Germans never again attempted major parachute operations during the rest of the war.

The fall of Crete brought the entire Balkans under Axis control. The years that followed were extremely violent. In Yugoslavia, where the occupation was combined with civil war, one million civilians would die between 1941 and 1945. In Greece, a resistance movement fought against the Germans. The price of Hitler's Balkan victory was high on all sides.

▶ Finnish troops stand over a frozen Russian soldier in 1939. Many Russian soldiers did not have the necessary equipment to withstand the severe winter in Finland.

5 The Eastern European Front, 1939 to 1941

KEY PEOPLE	KEY PLACES
Joseph Stalin	Russia
Adolf Hitler	Finland
Marshal Semyon Timishenko	
General Georgi Zhukov	

The German invasion of Russia was intended to crush the Soviet Union. Hitler thought that the Soviets were the enemy of Nazism. During the invasion, the Russians suffered huge losses. Yet they were able to stop the German Blitzkrieg.

After the defeat of Poland in September 1939, the Soviets stationed troops in Estonia, Latvia, and Lithuania. One month later, Joseph Stalin demanded that Finland give the Soviet Union a large area of territory. He wanted to safeguard his country's northern coast, especially Leningrad (now St. Petersburg).

The Finns tried to negotiate. On November 26, 1939, the Soviet foreign minister announced that the Finns had fired on Red Army troops. He demanded that the Finns withdraw 15 miles (24 km) from the border. Negotiations failed. Four days later, Finland was invaded without a formal declaration of war.

The Russo-Finnish War

The two sides seemed mismatched. The Soviets had around 300,000 troops and 800 aircraft. The Finns only had about 120,000 troops and 100 aircraft. However, the Finns were well trained and equipped to handle their country's cold winters and thick forests. The Red Army was not. Many Russians froze to death. The Finns used ambushes and guerrilla warfare to delay the Red Army. Then they fell back, destroying everything of military value as they went.

The Russo-Finnish War (1939 to 1940) lasted nearly four months. The Soviet Union took control of vast tracts of Finnish territory. The Soviets wanted to create a barrier between themselves and Nazi Germany.

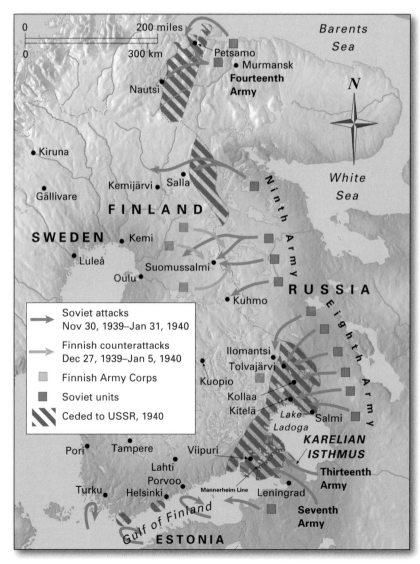

At first, the Finnish tactics and poor Russian leadership decided the outcome. The commander of the Finns was Field Marshal Carl Mannerheim. On the southern front, the Soviets advanced 90 miles (144 km) before running into the defenses of the Mannerheim Line. The Mannerheim Line stretched across the narrow Karelian Isthmus between the Gulf of Finland and Lake Ladoga and prevented the Soviet troops from advancing.

In the north, two Soviet divisions of the Eighth Army were destroyed by just 5,000 Finns. Also in the north, the Soviet Ninth Army lost two divisions. At the end of 1939, 27,000 Red Army soldiers were dead and many more wounded. However, the Finns had only 2,700 total casualties. Enormous quantities of Soviet equipment had been destroyed or abandoned.

Despite this setback, Stalin did not give up. He continued his plan even when the League of Nations allowed its members to intervene on Finland's behalf.

Despite this setback, Stalin did not give up. He continued his plan even when the League of Nations allowed its members to intervene on Finland's behalf. He increased the number of Red Army soldiers so they outnumbered the Finns three to one. Stalin also appointed an experienced commander, Marshal Semyon Timoshenko. The second Soviet offensive opened on February 1, 1940 and gradually battered its way forward. The Soviets pushed through the Mannerheim Line.

Although the Soviets improved their tactics, they continued to suffer severe losses. However, the Finns began to run short of troops and ammunition. They were spread too thinly to blunt all of the Soviet attacks. Eventually, the Finns realized they couldn't win. They traveled to Moscow to negotiate for peace on March 8.

The Russo-Finnish Treaty, signed four days later, forced the Finns to give Stalin large tracts, or areas, of territory that had been essential to Finland's defense. The treaty also called for the building of a railroad from the Soviet port of Murmansk through Finland's northern interior. The Finns had deployed some 600,000 men and suffered 68,000 killed and wounded. Official Soviet figures claimed around 49,000 dead and 159,000 wounded. The Red Army also lost 1,600 tanks and 872 aircraft.

Buildup to Germany's Invasion

After the division of Poland in 1939, Hitler and Stalin tried to buy time. Hitler wanted a peaceful eastern border. That way he could turn his attention to Britain and France. Stalin wanted to protect Russia's borders. So he took over the Baltic States and went to war with Finland. Stalin's intention was to push Russia's borders outward. That way, a German invasion would begin outside of Russian territory proper. That gave greater protection to key cities such as Leningrad and Moscow and Soviet industrial and agricultural heartlands.

Hitler, though, wanted to invade and crush the Soviet Union. He decided to do so in late July 1940. But his commanders weren't ready. So Hitler agreed to a date of May 1941.

Diplomatic contacts between the Soviet Union and Germany continued. Trade agreements were maintained. For example, Germany took raw materials from Russia, and sent military technology in return.

Hitler, though, wanted to invade and crush the Soviet Union. He decided to do so in late July 1940. But his commanders weren't ready. So Hitler agreed to a date of May 1941.

At the same time, German troops moved eastward. Relations between Germany and the Soviet Union began to sour. On September 27, 1940, Germany, Italy, and Japan signed the Tripartite Pact. This treaty was viewed with suspicion in Russia. Russia had recently won a brief border war with Japan. A few days later, Germany was caught shipping artillery to Finland. Also, German military advisers began operating in Romania, which the Soviet Union felt was within its sphere of influence.

Hitler became more committed to the invasion of the Soviet Union, code-named Operation Barbarossa. The buildup of troops in the east continued. Bulgaria joined the Tripartite Pact in March 1941. Russia wanted a non-aggression agreement with Finland and Turkey. It also sought to reach some compromise with Germany. At the same time, Hitler approved the final details of Barbarossa on February 3, 1941.

SOVIET-JAPANESE BORDER INCIDENTS

Between 1938 and 1939, tensions between the Soviet Union and Japan increased. A Japanese force, the Kwantung Army, occupied the Chinese province of Manchuria in 1931. It exploited an ongoing civil war in China. The Soviet Union was sensitive to such events as they threatened its Asian borders.

In July 1938, the Japanese attacked Soviet troops stationed at Lake Khassan, near the port of Vladivostok. After their initial advance, the Japanese began to build defensive positions. The Soviet Independent Eastern Army quickly drove the Japanese back into Manchuria. A second Japanese attack was repelled, but tensions remained high. There were further clashes during January and February 1939.

The following May, units of the Kwantung Army attacked troops in Mongolia. The Soviet Union responded by sending in large-scale forces under General Georgi Zhukov. Zhukov defeated the Japanese at the Battle of Khalkin-Gol in August. The Japanese opted to sign an armistice.

The brief war had repercussions. First, defeat made the Japanese wary of attacking the Soviet Union, even after Germany, its ally, invaded Russia in June 1941. When the Russians learned of this apprehension, they transferred many divisions to the eastern front. Second, Khalkin-Gol made Zhukov one of Russia's best commanders and brought him to the attention of Stalin.

General Franz Halder, the army's chief of staff, and General Friedrich von Paulus created the attack plan. The plan relied on Blitzkrieg attacks to catch the Russians offguard. The goal was to capture Moscow as quickly as possible before the harsh Russian winter began.

There were other motives behind the desire for a swift victory. Hitler wanted the rich agricultural areas of the Ukraine. Without these lands, Germany would have a hard time feeding itself if the war continued much longer. The invasion of the Soviet Union was delayed from May to June 1941. This was because Hitler sent his forces to the Balkans. That controversial delay would have major consequences.

The goal was to capture Moscow as quickly as possible before the harsh Russian winter began.

The final details for Operation Barbarossa were issued on June 6, 1941. The Germans positioned around 3 million men with more than 3,000 tanks from the Baltic to the Black Sea. There were also 3,000 German aircraft. Germany had the support of Romania, Hungary, and Slovakia as well as other volunteer units from Axis countries. In addition, there were five German divisions in Finland and eighteen local divisions. The Finns were eager to retake the territory they had lost in the Russo-Finnish War.

The Germans advanced in three Army groups along an 1,800-mile (2,880 km) front. The troops were supported by Luftwaffe air attacks.

SOVIET ARMED FORCES

STRATEGY & TACTICS

At the beginning of World War II, the Red Army was in poor shape. Although they had 3 million men and 10,000 tanks in 1941, the army was not modern or well trained. Its officers did not have experience. The fighting tactics the Red Army used were outdated. Germany's invasion in 1941 highlighted these deficiencies. In the first few months, the Red Army suffered staggering losses of equipment and men.

Stalin, who had little military experience, took charge in July 1941. In late 1941, a hiatus in the German invasion allowed Russia to rebuild its armed forces. New equipment, like the excellent T-34 tank, poured out of Russian factories. Britain and the United States also helped in rebuilding. Trusted, proven generals were given leading roles on merit.

As the German army grew weaker in early 1943, the Red Army grew more powerful. From 1943 to 1945, its divisions ground down the bulk of Germany's land and air forces. The Red Army's crowning achievement was the capture of Berlin in May 1945.

The Red Air Force had 18,000 aircraft in 1941, but many were outdated. Thousands were destroyed in the first few days of Operation Barbarossa. Eventually, more advanced planes were introduced. By early 1943, Germany had lost control of the skies over the eastern front.

The Red Navy had two main fleets in the Baltic and Black seas. In 1941 both were poorly equipped and badly organized. They also suffered severe losses to German air attacks. Because production was switched to other weapons, few new vessels were built. Larger warships supported ground operations, and smaller vessels carried out purely naval missions.

The Red Army guarded Russia's western border, which included the recently gained parts of the Baltic States, Bessarabia, and Poland. Some 3 million men were concentrated in three main army groups, which were known as fronts. The Southwest Front ran south from the Pripet Marshes to the Black Sea to defend Ukraine. Northward from the marshes to the border of Lithuania, the Western Front protected the capital city, Moscow. Extending from the Lithuanian border to the Baltic Sea, the Northwest Front barred the way to Leningrad. While the Russians had large numbers of tanks and aircraft, they were not the same size and quality as the Germans. In addition, the Red Army was poorly trained and led.

The Red Army's lack of preparedness and its surprise at the German's attack is one of the great mysteries of World War II. Hitler had hidden his headquarters in the dense forest in East Prussia. The Germans hid other preparations well. Yet the arrival of three million men on Russia's western border should not have gone unnoticed. Stalin was notified by Winston Churchill in April, 1941 that Germany was building up its forces in Poland. Churchill's intelligence was confirmed by Russian agents in Asia and central Europe. A pro-Soviet German journalist in Japan sent reports to Stalin in May and June. One of them correctly identified the date of Operation Barbarossa. In Switzerland, a network supplied not only the date of Barbarossa, but also some detailed operational plans. None of this seems to have convinced Stalin of the threat. Perhaps Stalin simply refused to believe the invasion was imminent.

This map shows the opening attacks of Operation Barbarossa in June 1941. German progress was swift, and by mid-July it seemed certain that the Soviet Union was going to lose.

Battles of Encirclement

Operation Barbarossa began on June 21, 1941. It caught the Russians by surprise. The Luftwaffe launched devastating attacks all along the 1,800-mile (2,880-km) front. As a result, the Soviet air force suffered huge losses. Close to 3,000 aircraft were destroyed in the first ten days of combat. Three great German forces pushed into western Russia. Army Group North drove into Lithuania to capture Leningrad. Army Group Center moved into the Russian-occupied part of Poland. Its objective was to take the cities of Minsk and Smolensk before heading for Moscow. Finally, Army Group South headed for the Ukraine, the great wheat-producing area of the Soviet Union, and the city of Kiev.

The German strategy called for rapid armored thrusts to pierce the Russian front line. The 2nd Panzer Group advanced close to 50 miles (80 km) on the first day. Similar progress was made over the following weeks. By mid-July, Army Group Center surrounded Minsk and took 290,000 prisoners. At Smolensk, 100,000 prisoners were captured. By this time parts of the army group were just 250 miles (400 km) from Moscow. However, the armies of the Russian Southwest Front fought back hard, stopping the Germans short of Kiev. Army Group North advanced into the Baltic States, where its troops were greeted as liberators. But its rate of progress was slow due to difficult terrain.

Hitler was concerned by the slow pace in the north and south. He transferred several units from Army Group Center as part of a new strategy. He did not want to capture Moscow before the winter. He instead hoped to capture the coal fields and to disrupt the oil supply to the Soviets.

Hitler's senior generals were shocked. Moscow had always been the key target of the campaign. The transfer of armored forces away from Army Group Center would slow its advance to Moscow. One tank unit was just 220 miles (342 km) from Moscow, but had to make a 600-mile (960-km)

Army Group North advanced into the Baltic States, where its troops were greeted as liberators. But the rate of progress was slow due to difficult terrain.

detour to help capture Kiev. The German commanders grew concerned about the soldiers' steadily increasing exhaustion.

Despite his generals' concerns, Hitler's plan initially proved successful. Kiev fell on September 19, with some 650,000 Russians taken prisoner. Other units from Army Group South reached the Crimean Peninsula. The Eleventh Army prepared to capture its chief port, Sevastopol. Closer to Leningrad the Germans had problems. Army Group North reached the city's southern and eastern limits in October, but the Finns refused to advance to seal off Leningrad from the north. This meant that Leningrad was not surrounded. People and supplies could get in and out of the city.

The German commanders grew concerned about the soldiers' steadily increasing exhaustion.

Operation Typhoon: Drive on Moscow

Even Germany's successes caused problems. Hitler expected them to be completed more quickly. Operation Typhoon began on October 2, when Army Group Center, reinforced by twenty-two divisions, struck eastward from each side of Smolensk. Again, there was a great victory. Russians were encircled at Vyazma and some 650,000 surrendered by the October 7.

By October 20, German forces were within 40 miles (64 km) of the capital. The Soviet leadership was near panic. Stalin appointed General Georgi Zhukov to defend Moscow. But the outlook was so bleak that the country's government operations moved to a town on the Volga River. Although Stalin remained in Moscow, the people were nervous. The invaders were near and the Luftwaffe made sporadic bombing raids. A decree was issued appealing "to all the workers of Moscow to observe order, remain calm, and give their entire support to the Red Army in defense of the capital."

Muscovites responded to the decree to a remarkable degree. Some 500,000 men and women set to work strengthening defensive lines outside the capital. Within a short time, 60 miles (96 km) of antitank ditches and 5,000 miles (8,000 km) of trenches had been dug, 180 miles (288 km) of barbed wire had been laid, and an additional 45 miles (72 km) of barricades erected.

In the meantime, two factors helped Stalin. First, heavy rain made the steppes into little more than muddy tracks. All along the line of the German advance, rivers swelled, making it more difficult for German engineers to repair or replace bridges the Red Army had destroyed. Supply columns were unable to move forward. Food, fuel, and ammunition ran short, but

Operation Typhoon, the final German advance on Moscow, began on October 2, 1941. Citizens of Moscow helped build 60 miles (96 km) of antitank ditches and 5,000 miles (8,000 km) of trenches for the Red Army.

Legend:
→ German attacks
■ German units
········· German front line September 30, 1941
– – – German front line October 10, 1941
— — German front line November 15, 1941
—·—·— German front line December 5, 1941
⬮ Trapped Soviet units
▪▪▪▪ Soviet defense line

did not halt the Germans. A Soviet spy discovered that Japan, Germany's ally, had no plans to invade Soviet territory in the Far East. So Stalin transferred twenty-five divisions from eastern Siberia to the Moscow front.

The onset of winter froze the ground and made traveling easier. By November 27, German tanks were within 20 miles (32 km) of Moscow. Despite stubborn Soviet resistance, a German victory seemed close. But the German forces were severely weakened by the intense cold. Troops lacked adequate winter wear. Equipment also failed. The German troops suffered severe losses by early December, including 155,000 men killed, wounded, or suffering from frostbite. On December 1, Hitler was informed that the German troops were exhausted and outnumbered. Four days later, Field Marshal Bock was allowed to withdraw his units to more defensible positions. However, his Army Group Center was stretched very thin over a front of some 600 miles (960 km) and had few reserves to call in as help.

The German troops suffered severe losses by early December, including 155,000 men killed, wounded, or suffering from frostbite.

Russia's Winter Counterstroke

The order to retreat came too late. Zhukov launched a counteroffensive the following day. Other large Red Army attacks were launched against German troops outside Leningrad and in eastern Ukraine.

Aided by overwhelming Soviet airpower, Zhukov's armies utilized their powerful T-34 tanks. The Red Army smashed into the German defenses, and most of the German units withdrew.

Stalin began to plan a greater offensive along the whole eastern front. Its preparation included reorganizing the Red Army and moving forces away from Moscow. Stalin's great plan did not come to pass as forces and supplies were exhausted. Nevertheless, the capital had been saved. Faced with the failure of his plan to capture Moscow, Hitler dismissed dozens of his senior commanders shortly before Christmas.

HITLER DISMISSES HIS GENERALS

The failure of the German drive on Moscow and the withdrawals along the length of the eastern front in December 1941 made Hitler furious. He looked for scapegoats and found them in his senior officer corps.

By Christmas, he fired his three army group commanders and thirty-five other generals on the eastern front. Among them were some of his best field commanders and many senior advisers. In a move that negatively affected the future German army, he sacked its commander in chief, Field Marshal Walther von Brauchitsch. Hitler placed himself as the head of the German army. Hitler would now dictate the army's strategy, even though he had no command experience.

Hitler had never fully trusted his senior officers. He believed that they did not fully support Nazism. The setbacks of 1941 convinced him that he had been right to suspect them. Eventually, several of the men he dismissed later returned to service as the war turned against the Third Reich.

The Soviet counterattack ended Hitler's hopes of a quick victory. From this point on, he fought a campaign against an enemy with immense human and matèriel resources. These resources could be boosted by supplies sent by its allies. Hitler realized that a huge part of Germany's more limited and severely depleted resources would have to be deployed against the Red Army. Large amounts of equipment were ruined. More critically, the German army had 830,000 casualties by the end of the year, roughly 25 percent of the June invasion force.

…the German army suffered 830,000 casualties by the end of the year

Hitler faced a growing strategic dilemma. He had declared war on the United States on December 11. Hitler knew the small but expanding U.S. Army would take time to arrive in strength, and that the Allies would need time to forge a coordinated strategy. But soon, German resources would have to be moved from the eastern front to western Europe or elsewhere. Still, Hitler remained determined to win a crushing victory on the eastern front in 1942.

▶German U-boats are lined up in a harbor off the Baltic Sea. The longest battle of World War II was between Allied sea and air forces and German U-boats trying to cut off the Allies' supply routes across the Atlantic Ocean.

6 The Battle of the Atlantic, 1939 to 1941

KEY PEOPLE	KEY PLACES
🇬🇧 Winston Churchill	Atlantic Ocean
🇺🇸 Franklin D. Roosevelt	
卐 Adolf Hitler	
卐 Erich Raeder	

The Battle of the Atlantic was the name given to the struggle between Germany's submarine force and the Allied navies and merchant ships traveling the Atlantic trade routes. These routes were Britain's lifeline. Later on, these routes were used to supply the Allies in the war against Germany.

The Battle of of the Atlantic was the longest battle of the war. It began September 3, 1939, when a German submarine sank a British passenger ship. Fighting in the Atlantic officially ended on May 7, 1945, when Germany surrendered.

If Germany had triumphed in the Atlantic, Britain would have been starved into surrender. The United States would have been unable to transport its armies to Europe. If Hitler had won, he would probably have won the war in Europe.

A Battle Above, On, and Under the Ocean

The Battle of the Atlantic was different from land and air battles of the war. Because the Allies delivered food, supplies, and troops across the Atlantic primarily by ship, sighting a German U-boat, warship, or German aircraft plane meant trouble. A history of the Battle of the Atlantic includes statistics on the delivery of cargo, the number of ships sunk by each side, and Britain's rationing system.

The ongoing battle was as harsh as any other of the war. The life of a U-boat crew was dangerous. They were terrorized by depth charges exploding nearby, they endured stale air, or they were crushed if their boat's hull gave way to the pressure of the sea. On the Allied side, a crewman on a torpedoed oil tanker might try to swim to safety from his ship. But he stood a chance of being burned as its cargo exploded and spread across the water. Or he might survive, only to die as a result of accidentally swallowing some of his ship's fuel.

This map shows the early stages of the Battle of the Atlantic, September 1939 to May 1940.

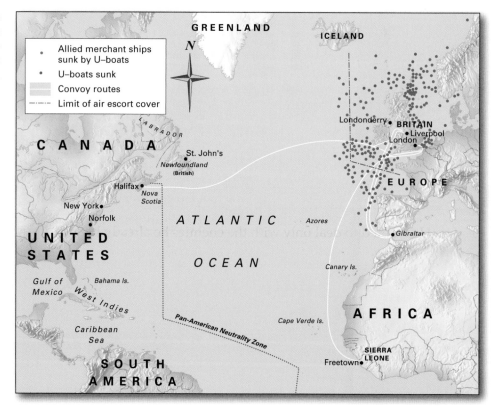

The Battle of the Atlantic took time to develop in intensity. Both sides lacked the equipment and the strategies at the war's beginning. Germany had only fifty-seven U-boats in service in September 1939. Some were not suitable for war, and others had to be use to train crews. The remainder would have to sail from Germany around the north of Scotland to reach the Atlantic. Hitler also ordered the U-boats to obey international laws and treaties. This order initially hampered them. Also, more than one-third of Germany's torpedoes did not work, which further limited their power.

In 1939 Britain had the world's largest navy. However, antisubmarine operations and Britain's naval air power had long been neglected. Too few escort ships could protect merchant ships, and as a result, many merchant ships were sunk.

The United States wanted to help Britain, but it was officially neutral. Neutrality laws made it illegal for U.S. corporations or the government to sell weapons to any of the countries at war. Also, no U.S. ship, civilian or military, could legally enter a war zone. Neither could U.S. citizens legally travel to war zones in foreign ships. The U.S. government established a Pan-American Neutrality Zone off the North and South American coasts. The U. S. warned that non-American warships could not enter the zone.

Initially, the neutrality of the U.S. prevented it from participating in the Battle of the Atlantic. Most U.S. citizens wanted to stay out of the European war. President Franklin Roosevelt agreed with his people, but he wanted to help Britain and France win the war if he could. As an important first step, the "cash and carry" law came into effect in November 1939.

Despite this U.S. bias in favor of the Allies, Hitler ordered his navy to avoid any incidents that might provoke the United States into helping Britain. He wanted to deal only with the enemies he already had.

Early U-Boat Successes

Prewar treaties and laws required U-boats to warn unarmed merchant ships before firing on them. Such warnings gave civilian passengers and crews the chance to escape before their vessels were sunk. But in the opening weeks of the war, there were a number of spectacular sneak attacks by German U-boats, such as the sinking of the *Athenia*.

After the sinking of a British merchant ship, the British immediately supplied merchant ships with guns. Merchant captains were told to radio for help if they sighted a U-boat. So, the Germans felt they could attack without warning. Although Hitler pretended otherwise until well into 1940, unrestricted submarine warfare began within weeks of the outbreak of war.

International law did not forbid surprise attacks on warships. On September 14, 1939, *U-39* attacked the most valuable ship in the British fleet, the *Ark Royal*. The *Ark Royal* escaped undamaged only because the German torpedoes malfunctioned. Three days later, *U-29* sank an older aircraft carrier, *Courageous*. Both *Ark Royal* and *Courageous* were being used in antisubmarine patrols. The next big German success was an even more substantial blow to British confidence. The main wartime base of the British fleet was at Scapa Flow, in the Orkney Islands off the north coast of Scotland. The narrow entrance channels were meant to be blocked by nets and other obstacles when not being used. The Germans detected a gap in the defenses. On the night of October 13, *U-47* crept into the base, torpedoed a battleship, and escaped into the darkness. When *U-47* returned home on October 17, the German propaganda machine trumpeted the success to the world. It said that the Royal Navy, for two centuries the most powerful in the world, could not even protect its main fleet base.

Establishment of the Convoy System

As soon as the war began, Britain introduced a convoy system to protect its trade. Convoys—groups of merchant ships escorted by warships—were a tactic of naval warfare for hundreds of years. Since Britain had more than forty merchant ships to each antisubmarine warship in 1939, it was impossible to protect trading ships unless they were grouped together. The Atlantic Ocean is so vast that a convoy was only slightly more likely to be spotted by an enemy submarine than a ship sailing on its own. On the other hand, a ship sailing on its own was virtually doomed once sighted by a U-boat.

TORPEDOES AND DEPTH CHARGES

TECH

Torpedoes and depth charges were the principal weapons used by the ships and aircraft in the Battle of the Atlantic.

Torpedoes are cigar-shaped underwater missiles. They can be launched from submarines and surface ships or dropped by aircraft. Most torpedoes followed a straight course through the water. The Germans had many problems with torpedoes during the first year of the war. These issues were not completely corrected until 1943. Torpedoes had a range of up to several miles. But, they were most effective at distances of roughly 700 to 1,500 yards (645 to 1,385 m).

Depth charges were drums of explosives dropped into the water by a ship or aircraft. They were fitted with fuses to set them off at a certain depth. They were not guided in any way, or fitted with any type of sensor. A single depth charge could destroy a submarine if it detonated within about 30 feet (10 m) of the target. Escort ships dropped groups (or "patterns") of up to twelve charges at a time, each with different depth settings, to improve their chances of sinking a U-boat.

A convoy of ships passes through an area of the sea. A scout plane returning from a patrol flight flies overhead back to the USS *Ranger*. Submarines successfully attacked relatively few ships because of the efficient work of planes like this scout.

The convoy system had its drawbacks. It caused delays and crowding in ports and other facilities. Ships that were loaded and ready to sail had to wait while a convoy assembled. Then they waited in line again when they arrived at their destination. The routes taken by convoys were usually longer and often in more northerly areas of the Atlantic than in peacetime.

Despite these problems, undoubtedly convoys were the best way to deliver vital cargoes. The first convoy actually left Britain the day before Britain declared war. But the shortage of escort ships and the huge difficulties in getting the system running meant that it was many months before the convoy system grew important.

At this stage in the war, ships were only convoyed for the first few hundred miles after the convoy set sail or was to return to Britain. A typical convoy of twenty or thirty ships might have only two destroyers as escorts, but even this protection made a huge difference. In the first nine months of the war, only four ships were sunk while in a convoy. Well into 1941, more than half the ships sunk were those sailing independently or those which had become separated from their convoys.

Shipping was important to Britain because it needed to import goods to survive. More than half of Britain's food and all of its oil were imported.

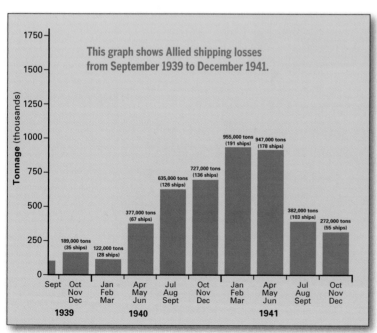

This graph shows Allied shipping losses from September 1939 to December 1941.

Other imported goods were vital to Britain's war industries. Before the war the British imported over 50 million tons of dry goods each year, but the rationing system introduced in 1939 cut this by about 20 percent. In 1939 Britain had the world's largest merchant shipping fleet of about 2,700 ocean-going ships of 17.5 million tons in all; the United States had just under half of that number.

Ports were also vital. More than half of Britain's prewar trade went through ports on the south and east coasts of England. This was because these ports were located near railroad hubs and specialized in technology, such as refrigeration. Unfortunately, these ports were the easiest for the Germans to attack.

The War Against Germany's Surface Raiders

Submarines and mines were not the only threat to Allied shipping. Germany had far fewer large warships than Britain, but German "pocket battleships" were a major concern. They seemed to have the same power as a full-sized battleship but one-third the size, making them very fast. In September 1939, before the outbreak of the war, two such ships slipped out unnoticed into the Atlantic. One of them achieved little before sneaking home in November. But at the end of September the other, the *Admiral Graf Spee*, began sinking Allied merchant ships in the South Atlantic.

In 1939 Britain and France between them had only five warships fast enough and powerful enough to engage the pocket battleships one-on-one. So the Allies deployed groups of smaller ships to cover some of the vast area in which the *Graf Spee* might be operating. In the next two months the *Graf Spee* caught nine Allied ships at places as widespread as the coast of Brazil and the Mozambique Channel in the Indian Ocean. Finally, on December 13, the *Graf Spee* was cornered in South America by three Allied cruisers. On December 17, believing that the Allied forces were surrounding the harbor, the captain scuttled the ship.

This action by the captain was the first of many times when poor German command decisions gave the British victories over Germany's surface ships. Later in 1940 and 1941, the *Graf Spee*'s sister ship, *Admiral Scheer*, and two battle cruisers were sent from Germany to attack British trade. They sank many ships but could have achieved much more. They were often frightened off from attacking convoys by a single British battleship. The battle cruisers ended up in the French port of Brest and were largely neutralized by British air attacks.

Wolf Packs and the "Happy Time"

Before April 1940, German submarines had limited success. They were in-effective because of the small size of the U-boat force and because their torpedoes did not always work. Germany's victories in Norway and France from April through June changed this situation.

The capture of Norway gave the German navy new bases from which to strike British shipping. But the campaign went badly for the Germans at sea. Many German warships were either badly damaged or sunk. At least forty U-boat attacks on British warships failed to do any damage because of faulty torpedoes. However, evidence from these attacks at last allowed the Germans to fix this problem.

France's surrender in June was even more important. Within hours of France's defeat, the commander of Germany's submarine force sent special trains loaded with technicians, supplies, and spare parts to the major ports on France's west coast. Shortly thereafter, the U-boats started using these ports as their bases. From then on, they could reach their operational areas

This map shows the Battle of the Atlantic, June 1940 to March 1941.

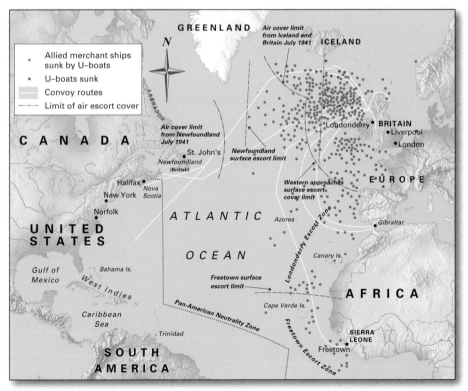

far more quickly. Italy also declared war on Britain in June 1940, bringing another large and powerful navy into the war on Hitler's side.The Allies were greatly weakened by the loss of the French navy. The British then had to attack French naval bases in Africa to make sure that the ships there would not be taken over by the Germans.

Up to this point the Allies were holding their own in the Battle of the Atlantic. The new developments changed many minds in the United States. The U.S. Congress agreed to huge increases in the military budget. U.S. defense planners always assumed that they would only have to fight one major enemy at any time. The most likely enemy in recent years was Japan. Now, the U.S. Navy would need increased forces to be able to fight in both the Atlantic and the Pacific. In July 1940 the Two Ocean Navy Bill was passed. This bill doubled the size of the navy. The increase in the navy was a precaution against Germany, but an unexpected side effect also helped to hasten the war against Japan. This side effect resulted because the Japanese attacked the United States before the new ships were ready.

In the summer of 1940, Germany still had about the same number of U-boats it started with. So, there were only eight or so in action in the Atlantic at any one time. British escort forces, however, were at their weakest level of the war. Many had been sunk and others were protecting their country against a possible German invasion or fighting the Italians in the Mediterranean. The result was that the German U-boats were able to sink 250,000 tons of shipping monthly at a time when British shipyards could build only 90,000 tons a month.

In the summer of 1940, Germany still had about the same number of U-boats it started with.

Faced with this threat, the British again asked for help from the United States. In September 1940, President Roosevelt made a "destroyers for bases" deal. He gave the British fifty old U.S. destroyers in return for leases on bases in British territories in the Western Hemisphere. He also received a secret promise from the British that if they lost the war, they would sail their navy to Canada rather than offer it to Germany. Further U.S. help for Britain would have to wait until after the November 1940 election.

The German submarine crews later referred to this period of the war as the "Happy Time." Most of their targets were still ships sailing independently. The U-boats began using new "wolf pack" tactics to attack convoys with more and more success. The U-boats now attacked on the surface at night. Sonar could detect a submerged U-boat closing in on a convoy, but at night a U-boat on the surface was very difficult to spot with the human eye. The U-boats slipped undetected right inside the convoy formation, fired, and slipped away into the darkness. They then followed the convoy at a distance through the next day and tried again.

Neither side had effective air support at this stage. Germany had some Condor aircraft that could patrol from bases in France to Norway. These aircraft helped by sinking ships or signaling to bring U-boats into action. Nevertheless, cooperation between the *Kriegsmarine* (German navy) and the Luftwaffe was poor, and few aircraft were actually used this way. In 1940 and 1941, the Royal Navy had few aircraft-carrying ships to use in convoy battles. The British RAF put almost all its longer-range aircraft into bombing attacks on Germany.

These aircraft helped by sinking ships or signalling to bring U-boats into action.

In March 1941, British prime minister Winston Churchill set up a Battle of the Atlantic Committee to coordinate every aspect of the battle. Significantly, the Germans had no such coordination. Admiral Dönitz, a junior admiral in the German navy, ran his submarine force with a tiny staff. U-boat building was low on Germany's priority list at this stage of the war. In February 1941 Dönitz's fleet reached its lowest level at twenty-two U-boats. However, sixty-seven boats and crews were in training.

In the fall and winter of 1940–41, the British gradually increased their convoy system. By April 1941, as more escort ships came into service, they were accompanying convoys for more than halfway across the Atlantic. At the end of May, escort ships were able to start accompanying merchant ships across the Atlantic. In May 1940 the British took control of neutral Iceland. The air and naval bases there were vital in this system.

The British also received a boost in March 1941 when six U-boats were sunk. New radar equipment played a part in these British successes. At the same time, the "air gap," the area in the middle of the Atlantic not covered by Allied air reconnaissance, was becoming increasingly important.

Enigma Breakthrough

The next major improvement in the British position also derived from their newly effective organization. In May 1941 the British began to decode radio signals exchanged by Dönitz and his U-boats. From May 1941 until February 1942, the British had an invaluable advantage in the Battle of the Atlantic. The use of the information was so well managed that the Germans never realized that their codes were broken.

The breakthrough by the British decoding service was made possible by a few brave sailors who climbed aboard a sinking U-boat that had been abandoned by its crew. They recovered secret documents and a German code machine, known as Enigma. The main use made of this information was in diverting convoys away from U-boat patrols. By late 1941 the Germans had more than eighty U-boats in operation, yet even with this force, the Germans found it increasingly difficult to find the British convoys. This difficulty was mainly because the British had broken the German code, which made a difference in the outcome of the war.

The capture of an Enigma code machine enabled the British to understand top-secret German orders.

The second half of 1941 was perhaps the most critical period for code breaking in the war. The Germans knew that the British would get some information from their radio traffic. But they had to risk sending a lot of signals for Dönitz to make use of his own intelligence information, to maneuver his U-boats, and to respond to sightings of Allied convoys.

In the summer of 1941, the British introduced new radio direction-finding equipment. Until then the best direction-finding equipment for getting a bearing on enemy radio transmissions could only be used on land, but by 1941 the British had adapted it for use aboard ship. This development had a vital role in the convoy battles for the rest of the war. For wolf-pack attacks to be successful, the first U-boat finding a convoy had to signal to bring others into action. However, if the escort ships could determine the origin of the report, one escort could drive the U-boat away while the convoy evaded the rest of the wolf pack.

Another important development was radar. At the start of 1941, some British aircraft began carrying radar able to detect U-boats on the surface.

Another important development was radar. At the start of 1941, some British aircraft began carrying radar able to detect U-boats on the surface. Few such aircraft were in service and their weaponry for destroying a U-boat was still very poor. In the summer of 1941, a number of escort ships ship received radar capable of finding submarines,even though the radar often broke down.

Later in 1941, the British gave convoys their own air power: a new type of small aircraft carrier known as the escort carrier. It immediately showed its worth. But the first escort carrier, *Audacity*, was sunk in December, and other escort carriers were not yet ready for service.

In the meantime, the British developed the Catapult Aircraft Merchant (CAM) ships. Fitted with an aircraft-launching catapult, these ordinary cargo ships carried a single fighter plane. Upon spotting a German aircraft, the CAM ship launched its fighter to shoot down the aircraft or drive it away. The British pilot then parachuted into the ocean, hoping to be picked up before he froze or drowned.

Sinking the Bismarck

In the spring of 1941, the German navy brought its most powerful battle-ship into service: the *Bismarck*, which represented the single biggest danger yet. Despite the loss of the *Graf Spee,* German ships had done significant damage to the Allies. Necessary precaution demanded that perhaps half of the British Royal Navy could be deployed, if even one German ship were loose in the Atlantic. Such numbers drained British resources.

On May 21, 1941, the *Bismarck* set out from Norway for the Atlantic. British cruisers located the Germans on May 23, and hurried to catch them. The first British ships in action did poorly. The *Hood*, pride of the Royal Navy, was blown up almost immediately. The *Bismarck* was damaged and headed for France. The strongest British forces searched for it in vain.

ADMIRAL RAEDER

Admiral Erich Raeder (1876–1960) was the commander in chief of the *Kriegsmarine* (German navy) from 1928 until Hitler dismissed him in 1943. In fact, even before Hitler came to power, Raeder was building up the German navy. After the Nazis began to rearm, Raeder developed a program to build battleships and other vessels to challenge Britain's naval power.

After the war began, Germany's strategy was dominated by the war on land. Raeder's ideas for developing the maritime war were often overshadowed. Hitler and Raeder had many arguments over how his ships should be used. The German loss in the Battle of the Barents Sea in late December 1942 sealed Raeder's fate. He was dismissed, even though Germany's problems in the battle were Hitler's fault.

After the war ended, Raeder spent ten years in prison for war crimes.

Admiral Erich Raeder

Two days later, British torpedo bombers located the *Bismarck* and made a last-ditch attack. They scored a hit that smashed *Bismarck*'s steering gear. *Bismarck*'s speed was reduced to a crawl and the ship was unmaneuverable. The next morning, May 27, the main British forces closed in and the *Bismarck* was destroyed. From that point on, the Germans relied on Dönitz and his fleet of U-boats.

The U.S. and Canadian Roles

Some of the changes in U.S. involvement, including the Lend–Lease program, were not related to the naval war but many were. The first important U.S. changes came in April 1941, when President Roosevelt transferred ten old U.S. Coast Guard ships to the British. U. S. permitted British warships to refuel and to be repaired in the U.S. Then the exiled Danish government announced that the United States would take over defending Greenland. Air bases and other installations were quickly built there. Finally, the president announced the extension of the Pan-American Neutrality Zone, roughly halfway across the ocean. Foreign warships—which meant German U-boats—inside this zone could be attacked by the U.S. Navy.

On May 21, 1941, a U-boat sank a U.S. cargo ship. As a result, Roosevelt extended the Neutrality Zone to include the whole of Iceland. Under the pretext of supplying the Icelandic garrison, U.S. Navy ships could escort vessels of any nationality sailing to and from Iceland.

By early September, the U. S. Navy had definitely started fighting.

By early September, the U.S. Navy had definitely started fighting. On September 4, a U-boat attacked a destoyer, which countered with depth charges. On September 11, the president announced that U.S. warships would "shoot on sight" in areas "the protection of which is necessary to American defense." Later in the month, U.S. ships joined the escorts of some of the convoys sailing from Canada to Britain, matching actions of the British and Canadians.

Hitler was still concentrating on the eastern front and did not want to provoke a full-scale war with the United States. Because of information from British code breaking, President Roosevelt knew that Hitler had ordered his U-boats to avoid attacking U.S. ships.

American help and the various developments on the British side meant that the Atlantic situation improved for the Allies in late 1941. November turned out to be the best month of the naval war. The U-boats sank only thirteen ships. Hitler also helped the Allied cause in the final months of 1941 by sending many U-boats to the Mediterranean.

In December 1941, everything changed with Japan's attack on Pearl Harbor. America was now at war with Japan and Germany. As a result, the British and U.S. navies were stretched thin. Resources were furthr strained with the loss of many merchant ships in the Pacific and Indian oceans.

American help and the various developments on the British side meant that the Atlantic situation was improving for the Allies in late 1941.

The year 1941 was a dreadful year overall for the Allied maritime forces. More than 1,200 ships were sunk. Britain's imports were cut by 40 percent. Reserve supplies were being quickly used. More tough times lay ahead for the Allies.

Allied sailors drop depth charges on a suspected German submarine. The depth charge would blow the sub to the surface. The sailors are protecting a convoy (*in background*).

▶ A German bomber plane, nicknamed "Fliegender Haifisch" (Flying Shark), flying over the English Channel, August 1940.

7 The Air War Over Europe, 1939 to 1941

KEY PEOPLE	KEY PLACES
🏴 Adolf Hitler	🇬🇧 Britain
🏴 Hermann Göring	🏴 Germany
🇬🇧 Neville Chamberlain	

Planes were first used in World War I to gather information about the enemy. Later, planes supported ground forces. They used machine guns and dropped bombs. Then the warring countries began to find that planes had other uses. These uses included bombing raids on factories and places with a high population. This tactic was first seen in German air attacks on London. These attacks were not very effective, but they helped prove that aircraft would play many roles in future wars.

The most important, single technological innovation of World War II was better air power. In World War II, bombing and air-to-air combat became common. Both sides wanted to control the skies.

Air Power, 1918 to 1939

World War I demonstrated the importance of air power in warfare. It was clear that in any future war, air power would be critical. In reality, air power meant the ability to bomb the enemy into submission.

In the decades after World War I, the nations involved in that conflict developed plans for air forces. The British Royal Air Force (RAF) was formed in 1918. It was the world's first air force. It was a military unit independent of both the army and navy. Quickly, the RAF developed new types of aircraft. Old ones were changed or phased out. For example, bombers replaced fighter planes as the basis of the RAF's fleet. Later, when Germany established its air force, the Luftwaffe, in the 1930s, Britain expanded its fighter capability. This proved vital in the Battle of Britain in 1940.

> *In the decades after World War I, the nations involved in that conflict developed plans for air forces.*

CIVILIAN MORALE

PEOPLE AND WAR

During World War I, the British people suffered from air attacks made by German airships. The German planes flew almost at will over the British Isles, their bombs causing considerable damage and loss of life. In June 1917, London was bombed for the first time ever by a large formation of German Gotha bombers. Such raids continued for nearly a year. Indeed, for ordinary people, this kind of attack was brand new, and the attacks caused considerable panic. The enemy air attacks also created feelings of anger, outrage, hatred, and a desire for revenge.

The philosophy behind this kind of attack on civilians was that a bombing offensive would break civilian morale.

However, British morale remained strong. In 1940–1941, the Luftwaffe bombed Britain's cities, leaving 30,000 civilians dead and many more homeless and injured. The attacks never broke the will of the people.

Historic Nazi Germany airplane Focke Wulf P-149

Strategic bombing is a type of air power. It was first described by Italian Giulio Douhet in his book *Command of the Air*, published in 1921. Douhet had many admirers, especially in Britain and the United States. He believed that destroying the enemy's factories and airfields resulted in air superiority. Conflict between fighter planes, he said, was a thing of the past. His ideas took hold in the Italian air force Mussolini established in 1923.

American William "Billy" Mitchell also believed in strategic bombing. He had been the commander of the Allied Air Services during World War I. After the war Mitchell tried to show American military commanders that air power should be used and improved. However, people were not interested in his ideas. Mitchell had to leave the military. World War II would later show that his ideas should have been considered.

After the war, Mitchell tried to show American military commanders that air power should be used and improved.

The French attitude toward air warfare was different. At the end of World War I France had the strongest air force in the world. But in the 1930s, French defense policy changed. The air force became less important. Instead, the French put money toward building the Maginot Line—fortified positions along the Franco–German border. France also began to develop its navy. As a result, when World War II began, the French air force was no match for the power of the German Luftwaffe.

The Luftwaffe was the creation of Adolf Hitler. It was equal in importance to the German army and navy. Hitler started building the Luftwaffe in 1933. This was in violation of the Treaty of Versailles. But Hitler didn't care. The Nazi high command viewed the role of the air force as support for their ground offensives, called Blitzkriegs.

The German air force saw its first action during the Spanish Civil War. Hitler sent about one hundred planes to support General Franco's nationalists. Some of the planes used the new technique of dive-bombing, which added to the accuracy of bombing. The tactic was infamously used in 1937, when German aircraft bombed the Spanish Basque village of Guernica, killing 1,600 people.

The Luftwaffe's planes were not meant for strategic air warfare. Still, Hitler decided to try to use them in the Battle of Britain. However, by December 1940, Germany's bombing campaign had failed to produce the desired results. Most of its bombers did not have good range, were poorly armed, and lacked the ability to carry heavy bomb loads.

Britain's Bomber Command

The RAF's strategic bombing force came into being on June 6, 1918. By the end of World War I, six months later, it had dropped 550 tons of bombs on more than forty targets, such as the German city of Frankfurt.

Disarmament and a poor economy meant that the air force, and in particular strategic bombing, suffered after the war.

Disarmament and a poor economy meant that the air force, and in particular strategic bombing, suffered after the war. The RAF slowly began to expand again in the 1920s. New squadrons were still equipped with aircraft from World War I. Not until 1925 did the RAF receive a heavy bomber designed for night bombing operations. These heavy bombers formed the core of what became known as the RAF Bomber Command.

In the autumn of 1937, RAF Bomber Command formed a plan in case Britain went to war with Germany. The main part of the plan would be a massive bombing attack on Germany's war industries. But in 1938, the British prime minister, Neville Chamberlain, stated that only military targets would be hit by the RAF. He added that the RAF would try to avoid civilian casualties. His statement caused much controversy. In the end, the only sure way to prevent civilian casualties would be to avoid attacking targets on land. Instead the enemy fleet, at sea or in harbor, would be targeted.

When the war started, RAF Bomber Command's strategic air offensive began—with the dropping of propaganda leaflets. On the evening of September 3, 1939, hours after Britain declared war on Germany, ten bombers, loaded with 500,000 leaflets, made drops over Hamburg, Bremen, and the Ruhr. These operations did not affect the morale of the German people. They did, however, have training value for the Bomber Command. They also revealed problems with navigational equipment. The leaflet raids continued on and off until they were finally abandoned on April 6, 1940. By then, Bomber Command had dropped 65 million leaflets on targets as far away as Vienna, Prague, and Warsaw.

BUILDING BRITAIN'S BOMBER FORCE

TECH

The establishment of the Independent Force, Royal Air Force (RAF) in June 1918 laid the foundations of Britain's strategic bomber force for World War II. The development of the RAF suffered in the 1920s from economic limitations and far-reaching disarmament measures. However, Major-General Sir Hugh Trenchard, the RAF commander, made sure that the RAF survived the financial cuts.

Still, expanding the RAF was slow, even though its future was assured. Originally, the RAF in the 1920s would be a force of fifty-two squadrons by 1930. Later this plan for completion was postponed to 1938. Only with the rise in 1933 of Germany and Japan did the RAF future brighten.

In 1934 rapid expansion of the RAF began with the new requirement for a force of forty-three bomber squadrons. With constant revisions to this number over the next few years, the emphasis shifted to the development of heavy bombers. The year 1936 saw the creation of the RAF Bomber Command. In development were the eagerly-awaited new monoplane bombers. This new type of bomber, such as the Vickers Wellington bomber, had a unique basket-weave structure, was only in prototype. Yet the British hoped that the bombers would be a strong deterrent to the growing air power of Nazi Germany.

This new type of bomber, such as the Vickers Wellington bomber that had a unique basket-weave structure, was only in prototype.

Britain's Daylight Raids Fail

Bomber Command did not just drop leaflets in the early months of the war. In the afternoon of September 3, 1939, armed missions were flying over the North Sea. One lone bomber took photos of German naval forces. This was the first British aircraft to cross into Germany in World War II. The photographs brought back showed three battleships in the Elbe River. A daylight attack was ordered twenty-four hours later by the Bomber Command. However, the attack ended in disaster. Five bombers were shot down. No damage was done to the German ships.

This Royal Air Force *Liberator* is parked on an Allied airfield, waiting to be loaded. Its payload of bombs is lined up alongside the plane.

The danger of sending bombers into enemy airspace by daylight became clear on December 18, 1939. Twenty-four bombers set out to attack enemy warships. They were spotted by German fighters. Twelve were shot down.

Clearly, if daylight raids were to continue, Bomber Command would face heavy losses. So, in September 1939, a new plan of action was drawn up. In case of a German assault on the west, Bomber Command would launch a large-scale daylight attack on the Ruhr. Such an assault into the heart of Germany's industries would paralyze its war preparations, or so the British thought.

The French disagreed. Air power, they thought, should be used defensively to support ground forces. Furthermore, an Allied attack on the Ruhr would invite the Luftwaffe to attack the French. The French air force was not strong enough to fight back. In fact, the entire Air Army bomber force in northeastern France was only seventy or so aircraft, all of them the old Farman 222s and Amiot 143s. Throughout the winter, these dated machines crossed the Rhine to drop leaflets and carry out reconnaissance, or spying, missions. As a bombing force, the planes were ineffective. So their activities were restricted to night operations. By daylight, their low speeds and weak armaments made them easy targets.

Such an assault on the heart of Germany's industries would paralyze its war effort, or so the British thought. The French disagreed.

British Night Bombing

In March 1940, Bomber Command began reconnaissance flights over possible targets in Germany. The goal of these flights was to report on how weather and other conditions affected what they could see. On moonless nights they could distinguish land from water at low altitude. In moonlight, areas of water such as lakes and larger rivers were visible from heights of 12,000 feet (3,600 m) and more. Smaller rivers and railroad lines could be seen from 6,000 to 8,000 feet (1,830 to 2,440 m). Towns and villages could be made out from 4,000 feet (1,220 m). Individual buildings could only be seen at a much lower level.

So, even in bright moonlight, bombers would have to fly lower than 12,000 feet (3,660 m) to see their targets. That was just too low to fly at night. The only solution was to find a way to illuminate, or light up, a target. A suggestion was to have one aircraft drop flares. The flares would then be followed closely by a bomber so that the attack could occur before the light of the flares died away. But the flares the Bomber Command had on hand burned very briefly.

Between September 1938 and March 1940, Bomber Command repeatedly asked the Air Ministry to develop new, longer-lasting flares.

Between September 1938 and March 1940, Bomber Command repeatedly asked the Air Ministry to develop new, longer-lasting flares. The Air Ministry argued that the flares they had were good enough. The Air Ministry also did not develop better radio and radar, which would have helped the bombers at night. But some research was devoted to developing more precise bombing aids, and the Air Ministry discussed the subject from time to time at conferences.

The Germans were quicker to develop radio aids. One of them was a blind bombing system known as X-Apparatus. It was launched in the spring of 1940. This high-frequency radio beam, sent out by a ground transmitter, could be followed by a bomber aircraft. A steady signal in the pilot's headphones told him that he was on-course, while a series of dots and dashes meant he was straying off-course. X-Apparatus was used in several damaging attacks on British targets before a way was found to jam the radio signals.

On April 9, 1940, the Germans invaded Norway. Bomber Command was told to attack German-occupied airfields in Norway. In the face of bad weather and without radio aids, the task was largely unsuccessful. On May 10, the Germans launched their Blitzkrieg in the west. Bomber Command's top aircraft continued their airfield attacks. Other aircraft were used in daylight attacks on the advancing enemy. Attacking centers of communication was another goal in this phase of the war. On May 11 and 12, thirty-six aircraft attacked road and rail centers around München-Gladbach. It was the first time a German town had been attacked by the RAF.

RADIO AIDS TO NAVIGATION

TECH

One of the first navigational aids used by RAF Bomber Command was a device code-named Trinity. This was a bearing and distance radio device that allowed an aircraft to fly along a radio beam until it reached a predetermined point over the target.

The idea was not new. The Germans had a similar system called X-Apparatus. It was first used when 450 German bombers destroyed Coventry, England on November 14–15, 1940.

The British used Trinity in December, 1941 against two German battle cruisers. Trinity was replaced in December, 1942 by a more effective device called Oboe.

"Pure" Strategic Bombing

The RAF Bomber Command was not given permission to attack targets east of the Rhine. This policy changed after German bombers attacked Rotterdam, Holland on May 14, 1940. That attack convinced the British that the enemy had begun a new kind of air warfare. The restriction of bombing to military targets was at an end.

The Command launched its first attack against industrial Germany on the night of May 15. Ninety-nine bombers were sent out to attack oil plants, steelworks, and railroad targets west of the Rhine River. Only a few planes located their targets. Even so, railroad junctions and yards at Aachen, Roermond, Cologne, and other cities were damaged. Airfields near the town of Duisburg, and Eindhoven in Holland were also hit. Heavy bombers carried out twenty-seven night attacks on German industrial targets over the next month. These rather uncoordinated attacks marked the start of a "pure" strategic bombing offensive against Hitler's Reich.

At the beginning of June 1940, Bomber Command thought it could wage long-range warfare against industrial targets in Germany. However, bombing strategy was dictated by the situation in France. France's land forces needed Bomber Command's help since its air force was so weak. The Germans were now masters of the French side of the English Channel. Phase two of the Battle of France, an offensive against the French divisions

HERMANN GÖRING

Hermann Wilhelm Göring was born in Rosenheim, Bavaria, on January 12, 1893. He joined the Imperial German Army as a lieutenant in 1912. During WWI, he transferred to the Flying Service and retrained as a pilot. In May 1918, after his twenty-first aerial victory, he received Germany's highest decoration for gallantry.

Göring joined the new National Socialist Party and played an active role in Hitler's Munich "putsch" in 1923. He fled Germany when it failed. In 1927, he returned to Germany and again became active in politics. In 1935, Göring was appointed commander in chief of the Luftwaffe.

Göring was very popular. But after the Luftwaffe's defeat in the Battle of Britain, he withdrew from public life. At the end of the war, he surrendered to American troops. He was sentenced to death by hanging at Nuremberg. On October 15, 1946, two hours before his execution, he committed suicide.

Hermann Göring

VICTORY

south of the Somme River, would soon begin. Then, with France on the verge of collapse, Italy entered the war on Germany's side on June 10. On the following night thirty-six Bomber Command planes attacked an airplane engine factory in northern Italy.

On June 22, 1940, the French government signed an armistice with Germany. Hostilities in continental Europe thus ended. The Germans now planned for the invasion of Britain. On July 10 the Battle of Britain began with attacks in the English Channel. The Germans followed the British attack with an assault on the RAF's fighter airfields. Bomber Command in turn attacked oil refineries and French ports where the Germans were preparing to carry their army across the Channel.

This map shows the main British bombing raids on Nazi-occupied Europe during 1939 to 1941. Beginning in May 1940, the British Bomber Command began to attack targets east of the Rhine, including major German cities and the capital, Berlin.

The Blitz on Britain

Then, on the night of August 24–25, 1940, the pattern of strategic bombing changed. Some German bomber crews mistakenly dropped their bombs on London. The British war cabinet had no way of knowing that the attack was in error. The war cabinet agreed that a raid had to be made on the German capital. On the following night, nearly one hundred Bomber Command planes set off for Berlin. The mission was hampered by thick cloud cover. The damage caused by the bombs was negligible. Most fell in open country.

Some German bomber crews mistakenly dropped their bombs on London. The British war cabinet had no way of knowing that the attack was in error.

No civilians were killed, but it was the first time that Germany's capital had been hit by a planned air attack. The effect on morale was tremendous. The surprise and shock showed in the faces of the city's residents. Luftwaffe chief Hermann Göring had given his word that no enemy aircraft would drop bombs on Berlin—and now it had happened. On September 7, 1940, the Luftwaffe launched its first air attack on London. Beginning at 5:00 p.m. and lasting until dawn the next day, 625 bombers pounded the London docks. Historians believe that these attacks on British cities was a mistake and probably cost the Germans any chance of victory.

The bombers then came by night in a new phase that was to last until May 1941. On November 14–15, 1940, 450 German bombers destroyed the center of Coventry. Night after night, throughout the long winter of 1940–1941, German bombers pounded London, the Midlands, South Wales, Lancashire, Merseyside, Tyneside, Plymouth, Exeter, Southampton,

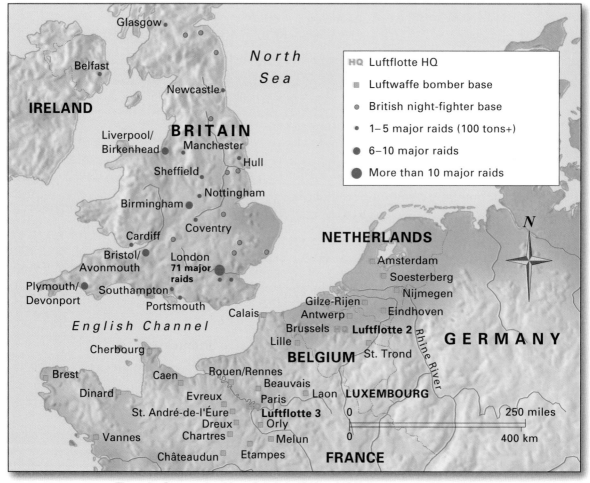

The major German air raids on Britain in 1940 and 1941, known as the Blitz. Although it caused heavy damage and loss of life, the Blitz did not crush British morale.

Bristol, and many other targets. The RAF could not stem the onslaught. The Fighter Command's night-fighter defenses were primitive. Most British successes had been with Spitfire and Hurricane planes, which were day-fighters. The British government feared that sustained German bombing of major population centers would in fact cause a breakdown in civilian order, but it never did.

On the night of April 19–20, 1941, the Luftwaffe launched a massive attack on London. Over 700 bombers were involved. Twenty-four were shot down. On May 3–4, 298 bombers struck Liverpool, which had suffered ten major night raids since August 28, 1940. The city suffered great damage.

Edward R. Murrow, the American CBS radio news reporter who was in London, commented after one raid: "I've seen some horrible sights in this city during these days and nights, but not once have I heard man, woman, or child suggest that Britain should throw in her hand. These people are angry. How much they can stand, I don't know." Stand it they did. So did the people of Britain's other cities, until the German night raids tailed away in May and June. Then most German bomber units were moved to take part in the invasion of the Soviet Union.

> *"I've seen some horrible sights in this city during these days and nights, but not once have I heard man, woman, or child suggest that Britain should throw in her hand."*
> —*Edward R. Murrow*

Meanwhile, Bomber Command continued to attack Germany. On December 16–17, 1941, the RAF first attacked a city (Mannheim, Germany) rather than a specific industrial target. The casualties were few, but 240 buildings, mostly houses, were destroyed.

Throughout 1941, part of Britain's attack was directed against German warships in French ports. These warships were a threat to Britain's sea convoys. New types of British bombers were also appearing. In of them was an aircraft with massive engines called the Lancaster. From 1942 on, this plane took the RAF deep into the heart of Germany.

In the 1930s students like these from the University of California, Berkeley, protested war. Many Americans, such as these students, were isolationists. They did not want to be involved in a war in Europe.

8 From Peace to War in the United States

KEY PEOPLE	KEY PLACES	
Franklin D. Roosevelt	Germany	Italy
Adolf Hitler	Japan	Spain
Neville Chamberlain	United States	
Emperor Hirohito		
Francisco Franco		

In 1936 Franklin D. Roosevelt was reelected U.S. president. He had achieved many domestic goals in his first term through his New Deal. Millions of people went to work for public works projects. Government agencies got involved in the economy to a greater degree than ever before to help agriculture and business.

The president's programs did not go unchallenged. They were sometimes opposed in the House of Representatives and tested in the Supreme Court. Nonetheless, a number of important pieces of legislation were still passed. But their overall effect was nothing like that of the first term. As a result, by Roosevelt's second term, the New Deal was running out of steam.

The United States was an isolationist country in the 1930s, unwilling to be involved with conflicts in other parts of the world. The growing aggression of Nazi Germany and Japan put pressure on the world view of the U. S. Finally, the Japanese attack on the U.S. fleet at Pearl Harbor in 1941 dragged the country into war.

U.S. Foreign Policy: Pressures on Neutrality

Throughout the 1930s, Fascist dictatorships in Italy and Germany and militarism in Japan threatened world peace. A string of incidents showed how real these threats were. In 1935 Mussolini's troops invaded Abyssinia (Ethiopia). In 1936 Hitler began to rearm Germany despite the Treaty of Versailles. Spain was engaged in a bloody civil war between Fascist nationalists and Communist republicans.

Since the end of World War I, the United States had followed a policy of isolation. Americans wanted to keep out of wars and conflicts in the rest of the world.

There were also ominous new treaties and agreements. Germany and Italy created a Rome–Berlin Axis. Japan joined the Axis in 1936 by signing the Anti-Comintern Pact with Germany, and later with Italy.

Since the end of World War I, the United States had followed a policy of isolation, as far as possible. Americans wanted to keep out of wars and conflicts in the rest of the world. Because of opposition to the League of Nations, Congress did not ratify the Treaty of Versailles. As a result, the League was weakened. This was one reason it had little effect during the crises of the 1930s.

U.S. public opinion remained strongly pacifist. In the spring of 1935, 50,000 World War I veterans marched for peace in Washington, D.C. Three days later 150,000 college students held a "strike for peace." In one national poll, 39 percent of all college undergraduate students said they would not fight in any war. Another third said that they would fight only if the United States were invaded.

Then came the creation of the Nye Committee. *Fortune* magazine had published an article about links between U.S. politicians and European arms manufacturers. In 1934 the Senate established a committee to investigate these claims. The Republican Gerald Nye, an isolationist, headed the committee. Nye concluded that bankers and arms manufacturers had tricked the United States into entering World War I. The war had been about profit, not freedom. The committee's findings seemed to reinforce public opinion.

WILLIAM E. DODD

William E. Dodd (1869–1940) was the U. S. ambassador to Germany from 1933 to 1937. He wrote to President Roosevelt in November 1933 and summarized his impressions of the Nazis and Hitler.

The Hitler regime is composed of three rather inexperienced and very dogmatic persons, all of whom have been more or less connected with murderous undertakings in the last eight or ten years. Hitler . . . is romantic-minded, half-informed about great historical figures in Germany and he was for a number of years a strict imitator of Mussolini. He rose to power by organizing elements in Germany which were partly unemployed and wholly indignant because Germany had not won the great war. . .

He has definitely said on a number of occasions that a people survives by fighting and dies through peaceful policies. His influence is and has been wholly belligerent. The last six or eight months he has made many, many announcements of peaceful purpose. . . . I think he is perfectly sincere and is consequently willing to negotiate with France. However, in the back of his mind is the old German idea of dominating Europe through warfare.

Roosevelt knew that the United States could not ignore events elsewhere in the world. But the president followed the national mood. He insisted that the United States would offer only "moral help" to the nations of Europe. The United States, Roosevelt told Congress, would be an example that would help "persuade other nations to return to the ways of peace and goodwill."

As tensions rose in Europe, the United States passed the Neutrality Act in August 1935. The act required the president, in case of war, to embargo, or stop shipments of, "arms, ammunitions, and other implements of war" to both sides in a war. Roosevelt also could limit U.S. travel on ships belonging to those countries. The act made no distinction between the aggressor and the victim.

In October 1935, Italian troops invaded Abyssinia (Ethiopia). The League of Nations protested. It asked members to place an embargo on all oil exports to Italy. The League needed the support of the United States. However, the Neutrality Act did not give Roosevelt the power to provide that support. Without the support of the United States, the League of Nations could only stand by as the Italians conquered Ethiopia. The Italians would control Ethiopia until 1941.

In July 1936 civil war broke out in Spain. The Fascist nationalists, led by General Francisco Franco, fought the Communist republicans. Europe's dictators gave military aid to Franco. Italy sent rifles and 70,000 troops.

The Italians successfully invaded Abyssinia (Ethiopia) in 1935 to 1936.

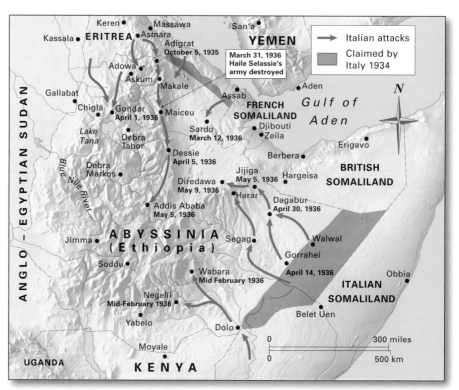

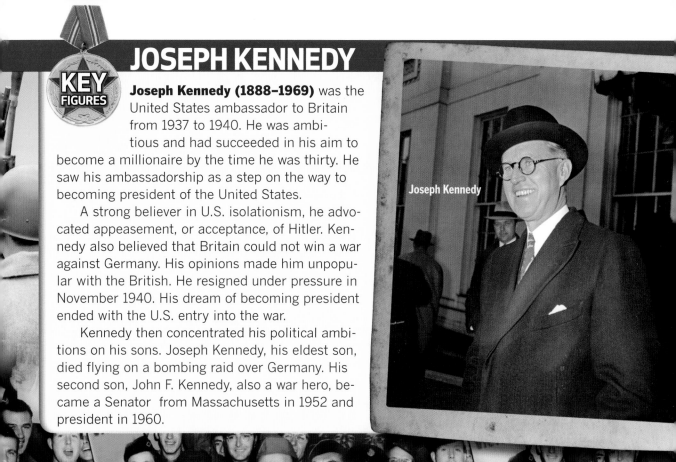

JOSEPH KENNEDY

Joseph Kennedy (1888–1969) was the United States ambassador to Britain from 1937 to 1940. He was ambitious and had succeeded in his aim to become a millionaire by the time he was thirty. He saw his ambassadorship as a step on the way to becoming president of the United States.

A strong believer in U.S. isolationism, he advocated appeasement, or acceptance, of Hitler. Kennedy also believed that Britain could not win a war against Germany. His opinions made him unpopular with the British. He resigned under pressure in November 1940. His dream of becoming president ended with the U.S. entry into the war.

Kennedy then concentrated his political ambitions on his sons. Joseph Kennedy, his eldest son, died flying on a bombing raid over Germany. His second son, John F. Kennedy, also a war hero, became a Senator from Massachusetts in 1952 and president in 1960.

Joseph Kennedy

Germany used the conflict to test its air force, the Luftwaffe. The Soviet Union, meanwhile, supported the republicans. Because the Neutrality Act did not cover civil wars, Roosevelt tried to impose a "moral embargo." He asked American companies not to supply arms to either side. His request didn't work. An emergency arms embargo had to be passed forbidding American military exports to Spain.

The U.S. public had little interest in the Spanish Civil War. Although some volunteers went off to fight, most Americans barely noticed it. Some people, though, wanted Roosevelt to change his policy to favor the republicans. On the other side, many Catholics urged support for Franco. They believed he stood for Christianity in the face of Communism. Roosevelt came to believe that the arms embargo had been a mistake. It had given Hitler and Mussolini power in Spain. At the same time, the republicans had become allies of the Soviet Union.

Meanwhile, in East Asia, Japanese troops had occupied China since 1931. Roosevelt—like most people in the U.S.—sympathized with the Chinese. The Chinese were seen as the victims of Japanese aggression. Japan also had great ambitions in the region. It wanted to establish a Greater East Asia Co-Prosperity Sphere. This ambition would be a threat to U.S. interests in the region, including military bases in the Philippines. Roosevelt believed that any embargo would help the Japanese over the Chinese. Since Japan had made no formal declaration of war, Roosevelt chose to ignore the conflict. This lack of action allowed arms to reach the Chinese.

The Japanese soon began to blockade Chinese ports. Roosevelt warned U.S. shipping companies that they were carrying arms to the region at their own risk. He did not want a minor incident to force the United States into a war. At a conference in Brussels, Belgium, in November 1937, the United States said it would remain neutral in the conflict.

That neutrality was severely tested the following month. On December 12, 1937, Japanese fighter planes attacked the U.S. patrol boat *Panay* in the Chang (Yangtze) River, an international waterway. Two sailors and a civilian died. Another eleven sailors were badly wounded. The Japanese apologized and claimed the action was a mistake. Later it became clear that it had been intentional. Their government was growing more aggressive.

Roosevelt took note. He saw that Germany, Italy, and Japan were all becoming more warlike. On October 5, 1937, he began to change his foreign policy. In a famous speech in Chicago he compared international aggression to a disease: "When an epidemic of physical disease starts to spread, the community approves and joins in a quarantine of the patient in order to protect the health of the community against the spread of disease." The so-called Quarantine Speech was a warning to isolationists that the nation could not stand apart from a general conflict. The nation might be called on to help end acts of aggression. He added: "Let no one imagine that America will escape, that it may expect mercy, that this

Roosevelt took note. He saw that Germany, Italy, and Japan were all becoming more warlike. On October 5, 1937, he began to change his foreign policy.

Western Hemisphere will not be attacked, and that it will continue tranquilly and peacefully to carry on the ethics and the arts of civilization."

In Europe, Hitler's ambitions grew. In March 1938, German troops marched into Austria. Hitler announced the Anschluss, or unification, of the two peoples. In September he laid claim to the Sudetenland, a German-speaking area of Czechoslovakia. In a meeting at Munich in late September, European leaders tried to prevent Hitler from leading the continent to war. They appeased him and accepted his demands in Czechoslovakia. Roosevelt said he was "not a bit upset over the final result." Roosevelt and the U.S. public hoped that Hitler's aggression was at an end.

Hitler expanded German territory from 1933 to 1938. German troops occupied the Rhineland, Austria, Sudetenland, and Czechoslovakia. President Roosevelt hoped that the German aggression ended with the occupation of Czechosolvakia.

Lifting the Arms Embargo

War broke out in Europe on September 1, 1939, when Hitler invaded Poland. Roosevelt was angered by this aggression. He knew that a victory by Germany and its allies would hurt U.S. interests and democratic values. European leaders expected little help from the United States. British Prime Minister Neville Chamberlain, said: "It is always best and safest to count on nothing from the Americans but words."

Roosevelt was worried that Britain and France would not be able to arm themselves quickly enough to stand up to Germany and Italy. He tried to get Congress to revise the Neutrality Act. He wanted the act to distinguish between aggressor and victim nations. In that way, an arms embargo could be applied only to one side, not the other. The first time he asked, Congress refused. After Germany's invasion of Poland, however, Congress repealed the arms embargo. It created a "cash and carry" law on November 4, 1939.

The new law allowed any country to buy weapons from U. S. manufacturers. However, the nations had to pay in cash, not with credit. They had to transport the goods in their own ships.

The new law allowed any country to buy weapons from U.S. manufacturers. However, the nations had to pay in cash, not with credit. They had to transport the goods in their own ships. Although the law applied equally to all European countries, Britain had naval dominance of the Atlantic. That meant the new law really just applied to the French and the British. Within days, both nations began ordering aircraft and guns from the United States.

Destroyers for Bases

In spring 1940, German troops overran Denmark, Norway, Belgium, the Netherlands, and France. Britain also seemed to be near defeat. If the British were defeated, Hitler would have a free hand in Europe. In response, many Americans changed their views on isolationism. In April 1940 the House had cut the armed forces budget and canceled orders for aircraft. But then the U.S. was faced with the prospect of having to defend itself against both Germany and Japan. So in July the House passed a huge increase in spending on the U.S. Navy. The Two Ocean Navy Act almost doubled the size of the U.S. fleet, in both the Atlantic and Pacific.

The British victory in the Battle of Britain in the fall of 1940 kept opposition to Hitler alive. The British had a problem, however. They were running short of money to buy supplies. Roosevelt, meanwhile, was running for a third term as president. The Republican candidate was Wendell Wilkie. He was young and popular. But Wilkie angered his party by supporting Roosevelt's plan to give aid to the British. During the campaign, Roosevelt promised not to send U.S. troops to war unless the nation was attacked. Meanwhile, British arms purchases and rearmament in the United States were creating jobs. Roosevelt won reelection, with 54.8 percent of the popular vote to Wilkie's 44.8 percent.

During the campaign, Wilkie had supported Roosevelt's so-called Destroyers for Bases agreement. Roosevelt did not present the agreement to Congress for approval. Instead he used executive authority to transfer fifty old U.S. Navy destroyers to the British, who needed to step up their efforts against U-boats in the Atlantic. In return, the U.S. was leased military bases in British territory in the Western Hemisphere.

THE *KEARNY* AND THE *REUBEN JAMES*

KEY EVENTS

As part of President Roosevelt's neutrality patrol, U. S. naval operations increased in the western Atlantic. These patrols inevitably came into contact with enemy submarines and ships. In mid-October 1941, a torpedo from the a German U-boat sank the U. S. destroyer *Kearny*. The destroyer was escorting a British convoy. Eleven Americans died.

One month later, another attack sank the U. S. destroyer *Reuben James*. This time, 115 men lost their lives. These two events made Americans suddenly realize just how involved the U. S. was in the European conflict. In fact, Americans were already dying in the struggle against Fascism.

Roosevelt used the two attacks on the destroyers, however, to call for amendments to the Neutrality Act. However, isolationists were fiercely critical that U. S. lives were being sacrificed in an European conflict. Officially, the United States still had no part in the events in Europe.

Wendell Wilkie also supported the Selective Service Act, which was passed on September 14. It introduced a peace-time military draft in the United States for the first time. Although Roosevelt felt that the size of the army should increase, he knew that a draft could be a political disaster. The U.S. Army stood at only 188,000 troops when war broke out in Europe. Roosevelt requested an increase of 17,000 troops. The Army General Staff, however, believed that the force needed to be much larger. Eventually, Roosevelt's secretary of war, Henry Stimson, convinced him to support the draft. The act allowed Roosevelt to call up to 900,000 draftees, selected from all males between the ages of twenty-one and thirty-six. They would serve a year on active duty and ten years in the reserves. The first were enlisted in November: by June 1941 the U.S. Army had swelled to 1.25 million, of whom 629,000 were draftees.

REGISTRATION CARD—(Men born on or after April 28, 1877 and on or before February 16, 1897)

SERIAL NUMBER	1. NAME (Print)			ORDER NUMBER
U 1756	Eugene	Buss	Abbott	
	(First)	(Middle)	(Last)	

2. PLACE OF RESIDENCE (Print)

182 E. Jackson   Painesville   Lake   Ohio
(Number and street) (Town, township, village, or city) (County) (State)

[THE PLACE OF RESIDENCE GIVEN ON THE LINE ABOVE WILL DETERMINE LOCAL BOARD JURISDICTION; LINE 2 OF REGISTRATION CERTIFICATE WILL BE IDENTICAL]

3. MAILING ADDRESS

Box 150 - Painesville Post office Painesville. O.
[Mailing address if other than place indicated on line 2. If same insert word same]

4. TELEPHONE	5. AGE IN YEARS 63	6. PLACE OF BIRTH Cleveland
		(Town or county)
Painesville 4680	DATE OF BIRTH Nov. 15 1877	Ohio
(Exchange) (Number)	(Mo.) (Day) (Yr.)	(State or country)

7. NAME AND ADDRESS OF PERSON WHO WILL ALWAYS KNOW YOUR ADDRESS

Rosa M. Abbott - 182 E. Jackson Painesville Ohio

8. EMPLOYER'S NAME AND ADDRESS

Self

9. PLACE OF EMPLOYMENT OR BUSINESS

E. Main St.   Painesville   Lake   Ohio
(Number and street or R. F. D. number) (Town) (County) (State)

I AFFIRM THAT I HAVE VERIFIED ABOVE ANSWERS AND THAT THEY ARE TRUE.

D. S. S. Form 1
(Revised 4-1-42)   (over)   16—21630-2   Eugene Buss Abbott
(Registrant's signature)

This example of a draft registration card shows that the bearer would be ineligible to be drafted. The Selective Service Act of 1940 established a peace-time draft. Only males between the ages of twenty-one and thirty-six were eligible.

THE ATLANTIC CHARTER

In July 1941, President Roosevelt had his first meeting with British Prime Minister Winston Churchill. They met in Argentia Bay, off Newfoundland in Canada. The two men issued a joint declaration about the objectives of the war against Fascism. The Atlantic Charter spelled out a vision of a world governed by democracy without war or conflicting national interests. The idealism in the charter did not sit well with Stalin. Although he was originally supposed to sign the document, he refused.

The America First Committee

Isolationism in 1940 and 1941 was led by the Committee to Defend America First. Its main belief was that the United States had no reason to fear the conflict in Europe. Right-leaning businessmen such as Henry Ford, a Nazi sympathizer, financed the organization. Its supporters included liberals and even the American Communist Party.

Among its noted supporters was Charles Lindbergh, the aviator. Lindbergh was a popular speaker for the committee. He argued that war between the United States and Germany would be a disaster. Around 80 percent of Americans supported the committee's stance that the United States should not declare war on the Axis Powers. However, Lindbergh greatly harmed the movement. He did so in a speech in which he said "the Jews" would force the U.S. into war because of their "ownership and influence in our motion pictures, our press, our radio, and our government." With that comment, he lost much support. In addition to that of Jews, he lost support of conservative leaders, such as New York's Republican governor, Thomas E. Dewey.

Around 80 percent of Americans supported the committee's stance that the United States should not declare war on the Axis Powers.

The Lend-Lease Act

The Destroyers for Bases agreement in 1940 did help the British, although it did not address the real problem of supplying Britain war material. Britain was virtually bankrupt, as Prime Minister Winston Churchill told the president. In December 1940 Roosevelt announced his plan for a Lend-Lease Act. Roosevelt compared the war in Europe to a fire in a neighbor's house. If you had a hose, he argued, you would lend it to your neighbor and worry about the cost later. Helping your neighbor would also be the best way to make sure that your own home would not catch fire.

Roosevelt then addressed the nation in one of his radio broadcasts known as the Fireside Chats. He said the United States would become the "arsenal of democracy." The U.S. public supported the proposal. It seemed to be another way of keeping U.S. troops out of the fighting.

The act allowed the president to "sell, transfer title to, exchange, lease, lend, or otherwise dispose of" equipment to any country that the president decided was vital to U.S. security. In other words, the British government would be able to get the supplies it needed now and pay for them later. The

This temporary machine shop was set up in a large automobile plant. The workers would use the drill presses (*shown right and in the background*) to repair tank engines.

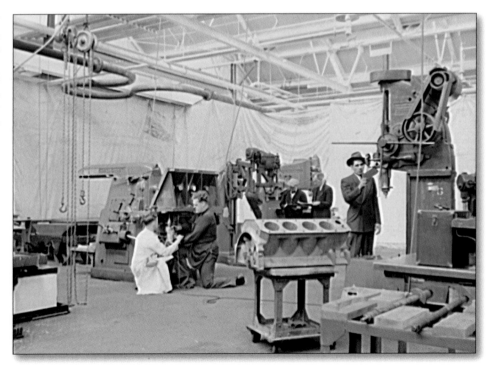

America First Committee and other isolationists opposed the legislation, but it passed relatively easily. In March Congress approved the first $7 billion for the plan. By the end of the war, historians estimate that between $13.5 billion and $20 billion worth of supplies were provided.

United States Involvement Grows

In secret, the U.S. government had long been cooperating closely with the British. For example, a series of secret discussions between U.S. and British commanders had taken place. If the two countries ended up at war with Germany and Japan, they agreed that they would first concentrate on defeating Germany. Then they would deal with Japan. The discussions also allowed the two nations to swap information. The British told the Americans what they had learned from German codes. In turn, the United States revealed details of Japan's secret diplomatic messages.

Meanwhile, Roosevelt was eager to transport Lend-Lease material to Britain. In spring 1941 he declared a neutrality zone that covered most of the western half of the Atlantic. The U.S. patrolled the area by ships and planes. They were to search and locate German U-boats and radio details of their positions to the convoys carrying Lend-Lease goods and to the British warships guarding them. Roosevelt next established Greenland and Iceland as part of the United States's "sphere of cooperative hemispheric defense." Both northern countries were close to the Atlantic convoy routes. The British had occupied Iceland in May 1940. Now, under a deal signed by the three parties, the United States would protect Icelandic neutrality.

U.S. Marines landed in Iceland in July 1941. Iceland, vital to the Battle of the Atlantic, provided ports for convoy vessels and also an airbase. The following month Roosevelt ordered the U.S. Navy to escort Lend-Lease convoys across the Atlantic. After the U.S. destroyer *Greer* was attacked by a German U-boat, Roosevelt ordered U.S. captains to "shoot on sight" if they came upon Axis ships.

Meanwhile, the Danish government in exile asked the United States to defend Greenland, an important stopover for Atlantic convoys. Greenland became home to air bases and other military installations.

Growing Tensions with Japan

Despite the war in Europe, in the second half of 1941 the U.S. focused largely on events in East Asia. The Japanese occupation of China was continuing. Japan and the United States were negotiating to bring the conflict to an end. At the same time, Japan wanted to continue to expand with its Greater East Asia Co-Prosperity Sphere. The Japanese saw the outbreak of war in Europe and the German victories of 1940 as a way to claim European colonies in Southeast Asia. Japan worried that more U.S. ships in the area might prevent this. Japan forced the Vichy French to let it move troops into northern Indochina, today's Vietnam, Laos, and Cambodia, partly to cut off the route for supplies to China. The United States retaliated in support of China. It embargoed sales of scrap iron and steel to Japan. The embargo was later widened to other goods.

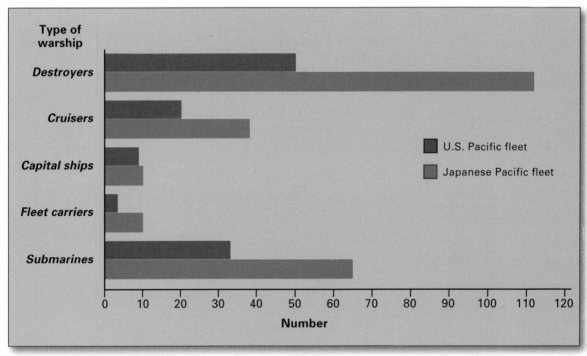

This chart compares the strength of the Japanese and U.S. navies before the Japanese attack on Pearl Harbor in December 1941. The Japanese navy was stronger than that of the United States in every category.

In July 1941, Japan's government decided to seize bases in southern Indochina. American code breakers decoded a message reporting the news. It sounded to U.S. politicians like the Japanese were prepared to go to war. Roosevelt then froze all Japanese assets in the United States. The British and Dutch did the same in their own countries. Roosevelt also banned the export of aviation fuel to Japan.

The effect of these measures was to cut off three-quarters of Japan's foreign trade and 90 percent of its oil. To some in Japan, this was a sign that the United States wanted to destroy their country. In the U. S. people did not believe that the Japanese prime minister could make an agreement that would be supported by the militants. When Japan suggested a summit meeting between Roosevelt and the Japanese prime minister for September, the Americans rejected the proposal.

Roosevelt then froze all Japanese assets in the United States. . . . Roosevelt also banned the export of aviation fuel to Japan.

In Japan, the government and the leaders of Japan's armed forces met with Emperor Hirohito. The government maintained that negotiations should continue with the United States. At the same time it ordered the army and navy to be at full war readiness. Early in October, the new prime minster, General Tojo Hideki, seemed to want an agreement with the United States. Japan's war in China was proving long and wearying, and Japan would have a hard time winning a military victory there. A war with the United States would probably result in defeat in both conflicts.

In the United States, messages to and from the Japanese ambassador did not ease the tension. The U.S. learned that the ambassador was not being honest about the content of the messages. The Americans grew nervous. On November 27 the United States ended negotiations and issued an ultimatum. It would sell oil to Japan only if Japanese troops left Indochina at once and China soon afterward. The Japanese could not accept such terms. On November 29, 1941, they decided that war was inevitable. Their plan was simple: to strike the first blow. They would try to take out the U.S. Pacific fleet immediately.

Pearl Harbor: The "Day of Infamy"

December 7, 1941, a Sunday, dawned like any other day. Army chief of staff George C. Marshall's wife was ill. They had a late breakfast in their quarters at Fort Myer, Virginia. President Roosevelt, suffering from a cold and headache, spent the morning with his stamp collection. Roosevelt's wife Eleanor was holding a lunch in the White House. Secretary of State Cordell Hull went to the old State, War, and Navy Building next to the White House. Japanese diplomats had asked him to meet with them.

December 7, 1941, a Sunday, dawned like any other day.

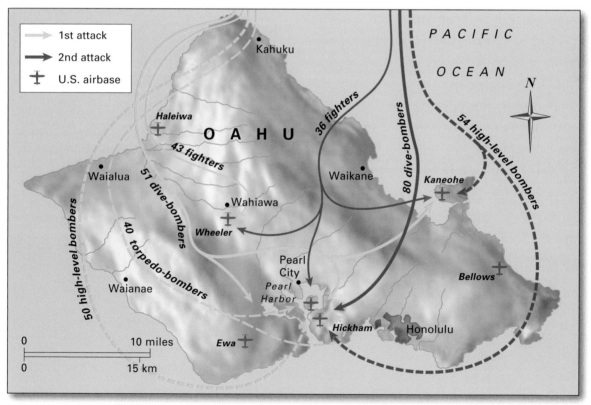

The Japanese attacked the American naval base at Pearl Harbor on the morning of Sunday, December 7, 1941.

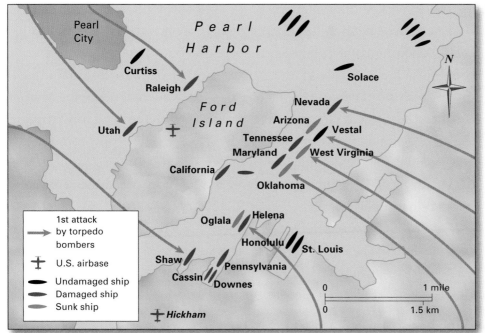

This map shows which ships in the U.S. Pacific fleet were damaged or lost during the first wave of Japanese attacks on Pearl Harbor.

The Japanese delivered the news that their country was at war with the United States. At the same time, their airplanes struck the U.S. fleet at Pearl Harbor, Hawaii, 7:55 a.m. (local time). About 360 Japanese planes were involved in the attack. Radar, new and not wholly trusted, had picked up the first 200 airplanes. They were thought to be U.S. Army Air Corps planes. The Japanese had planned the attack for early on Sunday morning for maximum surprise. The sleeping fleet was devastated. Five battleships were sunk, including the *Arizona*, which lost more than a thousand men. Three more battleships were damaged. Three cruisers, three destroyers, several other vessels, and 188 aircraft were also lost. The total casualties included 2,335 soldiers and sailors killed. More than 1,000 were wounded. Japanese losses were between thirty and sixty aircraft, five midget submarines, and fewer than one hundred men.

> *The Japanese had planned the attack for early on Sunday morning for maximum surprise. The sleeping fleet was devastated.*

News reached different parts of the country at different times. Federal Bureau of Investigation director J. Edgar Hoover received a call from his chief Honolulu agent, who held a telephone out the window so Hoover could hear the explosions. At 1:20 p.m. in Philadelphia, local radio programs announced news of the Japanese strike. Nationally, only the Mutual Broadcasting System interrupted its broadcast with the news, interrupting the baseball game between the Brooklyn Dodgers and New York Giants. NBC waited until its regular news broadcast at 2:30 p.m., eastern time. CBS made its first announcement before the 3:00 p.m. broadcast of the New York Philharmonic concert.

Due to time-zone differences, the news reached California and other coastal states in the early morning. Panicked citizens expected a Japanese invasion. In San Francisco a National Guard unit took positions on the Golden Gate Bridge. A widespread rumor said that a guardsman killed a woman on the bridge that night when she ignored his order to halt.

A small boat rescues seamen from the USS *West Virginia*, which is burning. Smoke rolls out from the middle of the ship where the most damage occurred. Two men stand on the superstructure above the smoke on the burning ship, waiting for the lifeboats to arrive.

People poured into the street. As evening fell, they started smashing headlights on streetcars. They threw stones at the flashing lights on the United Artists Theater's neon sign. Los Angeles officials called for all police to report to their stations. Individuals took to the streets, firing at airplanes and blowing sirens. FBI agents rounded up all known Japanese-American males and sent them to jail for several days. In Washington some individuals tried to chop down the Japanese cherry trees that line the tidal basin.

The next morning, recruiting stations were mobbed by men wanting to get into the military. Congress met and, after a speech from President Roosevelt, voted to declare war. The Senate vote was unanimous. Representative Jeannette Rankin of Montana was the only member of the House of Representatives to vote against war, a vote that ended her political career. Germany, on December 11, declared war on the United States to support its ally, Japan. The U. S. reacted by declaring war on Germany.

The next morning, recruiting stations were mobbed by men wanting to get into the military. Congress met and, after a speech from President Roosevelt, voted to declare war.

A question remains about Pearl Harbor. Just how much did the president and his administration know about it in advance? Some believe that intercepted Japanese signals had informed the administration of the attack. The warning had not been passed on because the government needed an excuse to get the United States into the war. However, most historians no longer believe this theory. Historians now argue that the United States thought that the Japanese might only attack British and Dutch colonies in Malaysia and the East Indies. That alone would have presented the country with problems. The U.S. would be forced into either declaring war on Japan or standing by passively. In the end, the United States commanders in Hawaii—Admiral Husband E. Kimmel and Lieutenant General Walter C. Short—were made to be responsible for the U.S. lack of readiness of Pearl Harbor. Both men lost their commands. They were punished for errors of judgment.

Timeline

1939
- Germany invades Poland.
- Britain, France, Australia, and New Zealand declare war on Germany.
- British RAF bombers attack German warships for the first time.
- The Soviet Union extends control over the Baltic states of Latvia, Estonia, and Lithuania.
- U-boat *U-47* sinks the British ship *Royal Oak* at Scapa Flow.
- Allies buy American arms on a "cash-and-carry" basis.
- Joseph Stalin launches a winter offensive against Finland.
- British warships engage a German pocket battleship in Uruguay
- Finland and the Soviet Union sign the Treaty of Moscow.
- Germany invades Denmark and Norway.

1940
- Winston Churchill replaces Neville Chamberlin as prime minister.
- The Dutch army capitulates to Germany. Britain launches its first strategic air attack on Germany.
- King Leopold of Belgium surrenders to Germany.
- Germans occupy Dunkirk.
- Germany's Operation Red begins.
- Norway ceases fighting.
- Italy declares war on France and Britain. Canada declares war on Italy.
- America sends arms shipments to Britain.
- Germany occupies northern France, Vichy France remains French.
- Italy attacks France.
- German U-boats attack Allied convoys in the Atlantic.
- The Battle of Britain begins.
- The United States signs the "Destroyers for Bases" deal.
- Luftwaffe begin the "Blitz"—the full-scale bombing of London.
- German forces enter Romania.
- Italy attacks Greece. British forces occupy Crete.
- Franklin D. Roosevelt is elected U.S. president for a third term.
- The Luftwaffe kill 500 civilians in Coventry, England.

1941
- U.S. builds "Liberty" ships to support Allied Atlantic convoys.
- The Allies defeat Italy at Beda Fomm and Benghazi, Libya.
- President Franklin D. Roosevelt signs the Lend–Lease Act.
- Axis troops take Benghazi, Libya.
- German, Italian, and Hungarian units invade Yugoslavia, capturing major cities. German forces invade Greece.
- United States troops occupy the Danish colony of Greenland to keep it out of German hands.
- Rommel's Afrika Korps begins the siege of Tobruk.
- Yugoslavia signs an armistice with Germany.
- The Greek premier commits suicide. Greek forces withdraw and surrender.
- The Allies' victories control the Suez Canal and Red Sea supply routes.
- Rudolf Hess flies to Scotland.
- The British Home Fleet later sinks the Bismarck.
- Operation Barbarossa begins.
- The United States bans the export of oil to Japan.
- President Franklin D. Roosevelt and Winston Churchill sign the Atlantic Charter.
- The siege of Leningrad begins.
- The Allies liberate Abyssinia.
- Japan bombs Pearl Harbor and declares war on the United States and the British Commonwealth.
- Germany and Italy declare war on the United States. The U.S. declares war on Germany and Japan.

Bibliography

Beaufre, André. *1940: The Fall of France.* New York: Alfred Knopf, 1968.

Bethell, Nicholas. *The War Hitler Won: The Fall of Poland, September 1939.* New York: Rinehart and Winston, 1972.

Bowman, Martin W. RAF *Bomber Stories: Dramatic First-Hand Accounts of British and Commonwealth Airmen in World War II.* Yeovil, UK: Haynes Publishing, 1998.

Churchill, Winston S. *Their Finest Hour.* New York: Mariner Books, 1986.

Cremer, Peter. *U-Boat Commander: A Periscope View of the Battle of the Atlantic.* New York: Berkeley Publishing Group, 1986.

Deighton, Len, and Walther K. Nehring. *Blitzkrieg: From the Rise of Hitler to the Fall of Denmark.* London: Triad/Granada, 1980.

Ellis, Chris. *21st Panzer Division: Rommel's Afrika Korps Spearhead.* Hersham, UK: Ian Allan Publishing, 2002.

Gilbert, Martin. *Winston Churchill: Finest Hour, 1939–1941* (vol. 6). New York: Houghton Mifflin, 1983.

Glantz, David (ed.). *The Initial Period of War on the Eastern Front, 22 June–August 1941.* London: Frank Cass, 1993.

Havers, Robin. *The Second World War (2): Europe 1939–1943.* Oxford, UK: Osprey, 2002.

Hough, Richard, and Denis Richards. *The Battle of Britain: The Greatest Air Battle of World War II.* New York: Norton, 1989.

Kershaw, Ian, and Moshe, Lewin, (eds.). *Stalinism and Nazism: Dictatorships in Comparison.* New York: Cambridge University Press, 1997.

Kimball, Warren F. *Forged in War: Roosevelt, Churchill, and the Second World War.* New York: Ivan R. Dee, Inc., 2003.

Liddell Hart, Basil. *A History of the Second World War.* New York: DaCapo Press, 1999.

Lukacs, John. *The Duel: The Eighty-Day Struggle between Churchill and Hitler.* New Haven, Connecticut: Yale University Press, 2001.

May, Ernest R. *Strange Victory: Hitler's Conquest of France.* New York: Farrar, Straus, and Giroux, 2000.

Monsarrat, Nicholas. *The Cruel Sea.* Springfield, New Jersey: Burford Books, 2000.

Moorhead, Alan, and John Keegan. *Desert War: The North African Campaign, 1940–1943.* New York: Penguin, 2001.

Murray, Williamson. *Luftwaffe, 1933–45.* Dulles, Virginia: Brasseys, 1996.

Mussolini, Benito, et al. *My Rise and Fall.* New York: Da Capo Press, September 1998.

Rommel, Erwin, et al. *The Rommel Papers.* New York: Da Capo Press, 1988.

Smith, Denis Mack. *Mussolini.* New York: Sterling Publications, 2002.

Speer, Albert, et al. *Inside the Third Reich: Memoirs.* New York: Touchstone Books, 1997.

Stein, George H. *The Waffen SS: Hitler's Elite Guard at War, 1939–1945.* Ithaca, New York: Cornell University Press, 2001.

Voss, Johan. *Black Edelweiss: A Memoir of Combat and Conscience by a Soldier of the Waffen-SS.* Bedford, Pennsylvania: The Aberjona Press, 2002.

Werner, Herbert A. *Iron Coffins: A Personal Account of the German U-Boat Battles of World War II.* New York: Henry Holt, 1969.

Further Information

BOOKS

Elish, Dan. *Franklin Delano Roosevelt* (Presidents and Their Times). New York: Marshall Cavendish, 2009.

Goldstein, Margaret J. *World War II: Europe* (Chronicle of America's Wars). Minneapolis: Lerner Publications, 2004.

Jensen, Richard, and Tim McNeese, eds. *World War II 1939-1945* (Discovering U.S. History). New York: Chelsea House, 2010.

Schomp, Virginia. *World War II* (Letters from the Battlefront). New York: Marshall Cavendish, 2004.

WEBSITES

www.wwiimemorial.com
The U.S. National World War II Memorial.

www.hitler.org
The Hitler Historical Museum is a nonpolitical, educational resource for the study of Hitler and Nazism.

http://gi.grolier.com/wwii/wwii_ mainpage.html
The story of World War II, with biographies, articles, photographs, and films.

www.ibiblio.org/pha
Original documents on all aspects of the war.

DVDS

Great Fighting Machines of World War II. Arts Magic, 2007.

The War: A Film by Ken Burns and Lynn Novick. PBS Home Video, 2007.

World War II 360°. A & E Television Networks, 2009.

Index

NOTE: Page numbers in **bold** refer to photographs or illustrations.